'I'm cold!' ...
Christie's ha...

'Liar!' she whis...

He clenched his fingers against her and laughed softly. 'You think you know everything. But you're wrong.'

'I have evidence, Lucas. My hands are actually on your skin. It's warm.'

Lucas worked the bedclothes free and covered himself.

'Now *I'm* cold!' whispered Christie, in mock-complaint.

'Then,' Lucas said in a low growl, 'you know what you can do about it!'

Dear Reader

With the worst of winter now over, are your thoughts turning to your summer holiday? But for those months in between, why not let Mills & Boon transport you to another world? This month, there's so much to choose from—bask in the magic of Mauritius or perhaps you'd prefer Paris...an ideal city for lovers! Alternatively, maybe you'd enjoy a seductive Spanish hero—featured in one of our latest Euromances and sure to set every heart pounding just that little bit faster!

The Editor

Jenny Cartwright was born and raised in Wales. After three years at university in Kent and a year spent in America, she returned to Wales, where she has lived and worked ever since. Happily married with three young children—a girl and two boys—she began to indulge her lifelong desire to write when her lively twins were very small. The peaceful solitude she enjoys while creating her romances contrasts happily with the often hectic bustle of her family life.

Recent titles by the same author:

STORM OF PASSION
BITTER POSSESSION

BLAMELESS DESIRE

BY
JENNY CARTWRIGHT

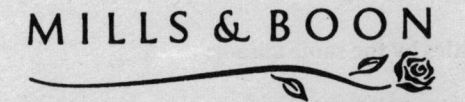

MILLS & BOON

MILLS & BOON LIMITED
ETON HOUSE, 18-24 PARADISE ROAD
RICHMOND, SURREY TW9 1SR

All the characters in this book have no existence outside the imagination of the Author, and have no relation whatsoever to anyone bearing the same name or names. They are not even distantly inspired by any individual known or unknown to the Author, and all the incidents are pure invention.

All Rights Reserved. The text of this publication or any part thereof may not be reproduced or transmitted in any form or by any means, electronic or mechanical, including photocopying, recording, storage in an information retrieval system, or otherwise, without the written permission of the publisher.

This book is sold subject to the condition that it shall not, by way of trade or otherwise, be lent, resold, hired out or otherwise circulated without the prior consent of the publisher in any form of binding or cover other than that in which it is published and without a similar condition including this condition being imposed on the subsequent purchaser.

*First published in Great Britain 1994
by Mills & Boon Limited*

© Jenny Cartwright 1994

*Australian copyright 1994
Philippine copyright 1994
This edition 1994*

ISBN 0 263 78490 8

*Set in Times Roman 10 on 12 pt.
01-9405-54336 C*

Made and printed in Great Britain

CHAPTER ONE

THE mirror was ugly and spotted with age. The face confronting it was very young and very pretty, though it was debatable whether the mascara wand being waved inexpertly between mirror and face was making the serious blue eyes look a scrap older or one iota more pretty. Christie didn't want to look pretty, anyway. She wanted to look beautiful. Svelte and sophisticated: that was the image she was searching for tonight. She sucked in her pink cheeks, and pouted her lips into a pretence of a kiss. *Seductive.* That was how she wanted to look. Mature, worldly and undeniably seductive.

She let out a huge sigh, then watched her lips press hard against each other in a frightened smile. Her blue eyes looked anxiously back at her. Tonight she had to make him notice her. No, she acknowledged, screwing up her eyes with desperation. Not just that. Tonight she wanted him to fall in love with her—to realise suddenly that she was the only woman in the world for him and to lean forward and kiss her with a dreamy sort of tenderness and then to... to make love to her. She opened her eyes and saw the panic reflected there. Of course it wasn't going to happen like that. Why should it? She was just a stupid kid. A stupid, completely inexperienced eighteen-year-old *kid*. A knuckle came up to dislodge a tear which was threatening the newly applied mascara.

She swallowed nervously, then looked back into the mirror, pushing her hair away from her face and forcing herself to smile a confident smile. The party should have started by now. She pushed her feet into her new and unfamiliarly high-heeled shoes and then resolutely turned her back to the mirror. It was time to go.

Squelch. Christie's frown dissolved into something more expressive as she felt water seep over the tops of her new white leather trainers. Reluctantly she peered down at her submerged feet. One thing only was certain—they would never be properly white again. Right now they were entirely obscured by the opaque brown water which oozed up out of the vivid grass.

'Mud...' she groaned, closing her eyes against the dispiriting sight. And then, with another resigned grimace, she turned to look at the tyres of her car. They too had sunk into the enticingly green roadside verge, almost up to their shiny hub-caps.

Wearily she squelched across the narrow sward to the metalled road beyond. With less than a mile to go it had seemed like a good idea to pull over, stretch her legs, kill some time, and give herself a final chance to think. It had been a mistake. This whole journey had been a mistake, come to that. She should never have let Aunt Sassy talk her into it. But Aunt Sassy was a tough old bird who, even at seventy—especially at seventy—liked to get her own way. Christie had eventually run out of objections. Now, looking down at the rich, clinging mud which had turned her feet into a pair of chocolate logs, she cursed herself bitterly for having given in.

Oh, it was all to have been so *simple*. She was to have gone to the house, taken a quick look around, driven down to the shop and shown her face to Maudie Timms, just in case Aunt Sassy checked, and then doubled back as far as Dursley and found a small hotel to hole up in for a couple of days. Once back in London she would have told her formidable great-aunt that it had been lovely, but no, on balance, she didn't think it was a good idea. Mission accomplished. Aunt Sassy silenced.

She stamped about foolishly on the roadway for a few minutes, hoping that her trainers would revert to their former splendour, but the mud clung as determinedly as ever. And the car, quite obviously, was completely stuck. She would only make matters worse if she tried to move it without help. Tentatively she leaned across and opened the hatchback, managing to extract an older, rather tatty pair of trainers—ironically brought along in case she fancied a muddy country walk. It was a very long time since *they* had been properly white. Tucking them under her arm, she set off towards the little stream near the church, where she could paddle her feet clean before donning her old friends.

Old friends. The village would be full of them. It was nearly five years since she had last been there, but none of them would have forgotten her, any more than she had them. Her plan most certainly hadn't included bumping into old friends. She had worked out what she was going to say to Maudie Timms when she asked, but what would she say to dear old Canon Percival when he asked? Or to Ellen Jefferies, who had let her have a go of her lipstick the year they were both fourteen and with whom she had shared all but one of her secrets? Or to Tommy and Malcom Brewer—or Mrs Brewer, come to that? Or—and her heart started to thump as the small inner voice whispered his name—to Lucas Merrick? What would she say to Lucas Merrick, if he should find her paddling in the stream?

He didn't find her paddling in the stream. Instead he found her climbing over the rickety fence at the bottom of the garden. She had figured that the best way to avoid old friends would be to approach the house from behind, through the woods. The fence had grown considerably more rickety since she had last clambered over it. It swayed and creaked beneath her weight, and she was glad when her slim, jeans-clad figure landed uncomfortably on all fours in the unmown grass. When she looked up through her thick mane of light brown hair it was to see Lucas Merrick framed in the kitchen doorway, watching her.

Christie closed her eyes tightly and dropped her head right down so that her forehead brushed the damp grass. She took a deep breath, bit furiously on her lower lip, then scrambled to her feet as if the sight of him meant nothing to her at all.

'Hi!' she called, waving cheerfully. 'Hi, Lucas. It's me! What on earth are you doing here?'

He seemed to stand extraordinarily still for a moment, but maybe it was only her eyesight playing tricks on her. She was, after all, utterly shocked to see him, right out of context, here at the back of the old cottage, where her one abiding memory was of her aunt emptying the teapot into the outside drain to avoid blocking the sink. In fact she felt quite brutally chilled by the sight of him— bloodless and faint. He mustn't be allowed to guess, though. He mustn't be allowed to know for one moment the effect he was having on her. She made her legs bound buoyantly up the garden, kept on smiling her cheerful smile, kept on waving. She ducked to avoid the sagging washing-line.

'Hello, Christabel,' he said at last; and his voice seemed to be at the same time very soft and yet very loud. It blanked out the bird-song and the whisper of leaves in the woods behind, and even, briefly, the thunder of her heartbeat; and yet its low resonance made her wonder whether he had actually spoken her name at all, or whether she had simply imagined the sound, rippling outwards on the still air. She was quite close now. Close enough to need to tilt her chin to accommodate his height as she looked at him. Close enough to see that his broad frame, casually dressed in worn jeans and an open-necked checked shirt, was as compelling to her gaze as it had always been.

He was smiling too, a grave smile which failed to touch the dark depths of his auburn eyes. 'It's good to see you again, Christie. There's no car at the front... When did you arrive?'

'Just now,' she said, halting her progress a couple of yards short of the doorway. She didn't want to get *too* close to Lucas. In fact her entire convoluted plan regarding this visit had been designed to ensure that she avoided Lucas at all costs. 'I left the car near the turn-off and decided to walk through the woods,' she added vaguely. She was reluctant to admit to him that her car was stuck. He might offer to help. Instead she gestured rather weakly towards the blustery blue and white sky 'It's such a lovely day. I thought it would be—er—nice. I'd forgotten the fence was so wobbly.'

He stood to one side, presumably to let her in. His expression was sombre, though the eyes which met hers as she brushed past him into the kitchen were enigmatically neutral.

'Still a little tomboy, eh?' he said drily.

'I'm five feet four, Lucas, and twenty-three years old. I'm neither a tomboy these days, nor so little.'

Oh, dear. She really ought not to have said that—especially in such an awful, brittle tone. She needed to keep things bright and breezy, as if... well, as if their meeting like this was very ordinary and everydayish. References to the fact that she was no longer a child did not fall into that category. Hurriedly she added sarcastically, 'Just because I'm not a decrepit six-foot giant like you doesn't mean that I'm stuck in some never-never land of perpetual infancy, you know.'

'I think I managed to work that one out a long time ago, Christie. And I should imagine you've managed to pack a fair bit of *maturity* into the past few years, now, haven't you?'

'Yes,' she agreed brightly, not letting herself wonder exactly what he meant by that. 'Well, of course I'm older and wiser than I used to be... It's only natural. Aren't you, Lucas?'

He didn't reply, and as she had marched on ahead of him she wasn't able to read his response from his expression. She didn't much like the silence, though. It seemed dangerous.

'What are you doing here, anyway?' she ventured lightly as she crossed the old-fashioned kitchen and went through into the sitting-room. Every object she passed— the chairs and the cushions and the plates on the wall— was warmly familiar. She would have liked to greet the old place properly, touching and looking and exclaiming before saying goodbye to it all forever. But she was far too conscious of Lucas pacing steadily behind her to pause.

He nodded gravely at the fireplace, where logs spat and smoked in the grate. 'I heard you were coming. The house has been shut up all winter. I thought it might be damp. I have a key, so I decided to air the place through.'

How had he known? Oh, Maudie, no doubt... Her aunt would have rung... Secrets were very hard to keep in a village like this—which was exactly why she'd been hoping to slip in and out unobserved. Fat chance.

'Oh. Right. I see. Er—thank you, Lucas. That was very thoughtful of you.' Her tone of voice, she realised uncomfortably, hadn't exactly sounded convincing. So she turned to look at him, offering him a weak smile of gratitude by way of compensation.

But he didn't smile back. He just looked very intently at her, and then deliberately and insolently turned his head to look out of the window.

'I wouldn't have bothered if I'd known you weren't bringing the child with you,' he said offhandedly.

Christie swallowed hard. The question couldn't be far off now that he had mentioned... the child. It sounded so stiff, so formal, put like that. The child. It hurt.

'Er—no. I thought it would be best... Well, that is, she's staying with Letty and the aunts, you see. They love to have her and she adores them and I thought it would be good for her to...to...' She tailed off. Her eyes travelled to the piano, on which resided a large collection of photographs in assorted frames. At the front were five or six pictures of the child. Christie's child. They had elbowed the photographs of Christie as a little girl well to the sidelines.

'You don't have to explain yourself to me,' said Lucas curtly, his voice suddenly suffused with annoyance. 'It's absolutely none of my business what you choose to do with your offspring. It simply occurred to me that if there was a possibility of a youngster sleeping in the house then it might be a sensible precaution to give it an airing.'

Christie felt a warm colour wash over her face. She turned to Lucas, her eyes a very bright blue. 'She has a *name*, you know,' she said tightly, trying unsuccessfully to keep the emotion out of her voice. 'Sarah. She's a little girl and she's called Sarah. She's not just a...a youngster. A nameless offspring.' And she waved her hand vaguely at the photographs.

Lucas glanced at them briefly without any apparent interest. 'She looks like you,' he said with manifest indifference.

'Yes,' She swallowed hard. 'Yes, everyone says that...' she muttered, her heart beginning to race. Now. He would ask now, surely?

But Lucas merely shrugged carelessly and then said harshly, 'Why have you come here, Christie? Have you come to pack up? Are you putting the house on the market? Is that it?'

Christie looked at the taut figure, outlined against the dusty lattice of the window, his head turned slightly away from her. As she looked he raised one hand and pushed his thick, straight hair back from his face. There was something terse in the gesture. Something that she hadn't seen in Lucas before. His lips made a thin, hard line; his eyebrows were drawn downwards in the middle. She remembered the way his square jaw had always lifted when he spoke, as if to let his words catch the sun, and the wry scrutiny of his dark eyes and the frequent fleeting smiles which had transformed the naturally hard outlines of his features into something dangerously irreverent, entirely challenging. She had seen him angry, too, many times. But never staunchly cold as he was now.

'I'm here for a variety of reasons,' she said carefully. 'Nothing is settled yet.'

'A variety of reasons? Like what...?'

'Why do you want to know, Lucas?' she asked, in exasperation. She moved her head brusquely as she spoke, shaking her thick, side-swept fringe clear of her eyes. He would ask soon—he must do—and she still didn't know what she would say...

There was a forced indolence in the way he turned away from the window to face her. With the light behind him his face was in shadow, but all she needed to know of his attitude was written in his posture. His hands had found their way to the waistband of his jeans, and his thumbs had hooked themselves contemptuously into his belt. He despised her. She was as sure of it now as she had been when she had seen him the last time.

'Your aunt is an old friend of mine. A neighbour. A *respected* member of our community. Naturally I'm interested in what you may be planning to do with *her* property.'

She looked sharply to one side, the tightening of the small muscles around her mouth registering her fury. 'You're being unnecessarily offensive, Lucas,' she said. 'You can choose to think what you like of me—and no doubt you think you've got reason enough to condemn me. I shan't argue the toss over that. But don't you *dare* accuse me of bringing shame upon my aunt, please. Nor suggest that I'm not to be trusted with her property. Aunt Sassy is proud of me, and even prouder of Sarah. All of her friends in the village sent me flowers and cards when she was born. Quite a few of them remember her birthday. My aunt and my daughter can both hold their heads up in this community. And I intend to do the same.'

'Then if you're so proud of yourself, how come you've not been back here before? How come your aunt had to make do with photos? Why did you never give her the chance to take a stroll through the village, head held high, pushing the pram? And why not drive right up to the house, for goodness' sake, Christie? Why come creeping in the back way? I thought you were a damned sheep, for crying out loud!'

Christie's eyes flashed. His accusations hurt. She had felt guilty at turning down her aunt's many invitations, but she could hardly spell out her real reason for staying away to *Lucas*... 'I didn't come creeping in the back way,' she insisted dishonestly, her teeth clenched. 'I told you. I fancied a walk. For old times' sake. Isn't the black sheep entitled to feel nostalgic once in a while? Or is such a pure emotion reserved for the common herd?'

'Flock...' he corrected swiftly.

Oh, damn it. She'd gone and amused him... His jaw lifted slightly and one of those smiles flashed across his surly countenance, making such mischief with his features that her stomach knotted with the old excitement. She scuffled her shabby trainers and looked down at them. Old friends... Huh.

'Then why,' persisted Lucas, 'if you insist that there's nothing hole-and-cornerish about this visit, won't you tell me why you're here?'

'What I choose to do is none of *your* business, is it? Any more than Sarah is *your* business...' she returned defiantly, unable to resist throwing his own words back at him.

Lucas sighed heavily.

She had been expecting a more spirited response. Instead he placed one hand over his mouth and drew his thumb and forefinger down from cheekbone to jaw before letting his hand drop. Christie noticed that his fingertips had traced lines, one scoring each cheek, which had not been there when she had last seen him. He would be, what? Thirty-four, thirty-five now? He looked even older. His thick, dark hair, pushed carelessly back from his face, revealed fine lines not just in his cheeks but across his forehead, and around those keen mahogany eyes of his. His dark eyebrows were drawn together in a way that was unfamiliar, too. The Lucas she remembered from her childhood—the Lucas in his teens, the Lucas she had seen every summer without fail until he reached his thirties—had frowned as frequently as he had smiled. But the frowns had been transient—a brief reminder of the sharp acuity of his lively, critical mind. This enduring harsh sobriety was new.

Christie turned away from him and looked resolutely into the fire. The logs were beginning to flare with more vigour; the smoke which curled up from them was less green and damp.

'Thanks again for lighting the fire, Lucas,' she said dully. 'It was a kind thought.' A prosaic thought. A sensible precaution. Not the sort of thing she had ever associated with this man. Time had wrought its changes on Christie. Why should she have thought that Lucas Merrick would be immune?

There was a silence, and then, as if cued to commence polite conversation, he said, 'And how is your aunt keeping?'

'Sassy? Oh, pretty well, though she has to walk with a frame now.' Christie let out a sigh. He would not ask now. Not while they were talking like this.

'Is she enjoying city life?'

Still watching the fire, unable to bear the sight of his face as they pursued this stiff, unnaturally formal conversation, she replied, 'She is, actually. She enjoys having Aunt Irene and Letty for company, of course, and she likes all the shops.'

'Good. Everyone here misses her very much. But they'll all be pleased to know that she's happy. Time moves on, after all.'

'Yes,' said Christie and her eyes focused so hard upon the flames that they danced in a mad blur in front of her eyes. She could feel a frustration gathering somewhere inside. Suddenly she blurted out, 'It's certainly moved on for you, Lucas. When I made that remark about you being older and wiser I thought I was joking. To be honest, I couldn't imagine you ever seeming old or wise.' There was a bitter little pause and then she added, 'Though I had no idea that wisdom made people so very dull. You were always full of surprises, but this conversation is the most surprising of all. You were the last person in all the world I would have imagined calling *me* a black sheep.'

Lucas surveyed her coolly. 'You made the remark yourself, Christie.'

'Oh... Did I? Well, you could have contradicted me.'

'Why? I know nothing at all about you these days.'

She dragged one toe irritably back and forwards across the hearthrug. Why had she gone and said all that? Lucas was giving off even more disapproving vibes now. And yet he still hadn't asked. What was the matter? Didn't he want to know?

'Christie?' There was a burr to his voice now which, like the lines, was new.

'Yes?'

She felt him close on her from behind. She couldn't tell whether she had heard his footsteps on the worn rug, or simply sensed the air moving. All she knew was that she was desperately aware of him coming up behind her. She flinched as his hands came to rest on her shoulders. She could feel his breath, sighing across the top of her head.

'Christie?' he said again. 'There's something I need to know...'

'Fire away,' she said brightly, as if nothing he asked could possibly matter to her. She kept her eyes glued to the flames. Oh, this was absurd. She could feel a tight, false little smile dragging at her features like a dreadful facial paralysis. And yet the mere presence of his hands on her shoulders was arousing her sexually in the most blatant manner. She folded her arms tightly across her breasts, pressing hard against them, trying to quell the unmistakable surge of desire which had set them tingling, and which had pricked her nipples into hard points— points which were clearly visible through the thin cotton of her sweatshirt. Locked in this ridiculous posture, her face fraudulent, her breasts unspeakably honest, she was going to have to try to answer a question she had been dreading for more than four years. And she *still* didn't know what her answer should be.

'Is there a man, Christie? I mean *now* ... A man ...? Important to you, I mean.'

Christie was taken aback. Of all things, she had not expected him to ask that. Her head swung round to look up at him. 'I... No. Why do you ask?'

His unexpected response was to bring his mouth down on hers and to kiss her, his hands twisting her around to face him as his mouth covered hers. Christie's eyes opened wide with alarm. There was something profoundly disturbing about the kiss. His mouth was questing, probing, as if it needed to know something that words alone couldn't tell him. Frightened, Christie kept her arms firmly crossed in front of her, forcing an uncomfortable space between them, and she kept her own mouth closed despite the rapid heightening of her arousal. One knee buckled treacherously, so that she leaned heavily against him. The brief contact of his thigh against hers sent shock-waves of desire rocking through her. This was intolerable. She jerked her head back hard. She *couldn't*... No, it would be impossible... She *mustn't* let him do this to her.

'No, Lucas...' Her protest was no more than a croak, but it had its effect.

Lucas let his hands drop to his side and stood back. He scrutinised her purposefully, his dark eyes raking over her, as if he would be able to see whatever it was that his mouth had sought if only he looked hard enough. And then he turned. 'Goodbye, Christie,' he said, walking swiftly to the door and letting himself out.

As the door closed Christie let out a hiccuping sob. There had been something so very contemptuous in the way he had kissed her—had said goodbye. And he hadn't asked, after all. It hurt her more sharply than she would have imagined possible. And yet how could she blame him for his indifference? It was all her own doing... all her own stupid fault.

It took a long time for the logs to burn down. Christie knelt on the rug, her eyes watching them blindly, her heart burning in concert as all those past summers— summers in which Lucas Merrick had figured so very large in her juvenile mind—tumbled in a glorious medley past her mind's eye.

Christie's mother had died in childbirth. Her mother herself had been orphaned as a child, and had been brought up here in the cottage by her aunt. When history repeated itself Sassy had offered to take Christie, too. But Christie's father, a schoolmaster at a boys' boarding-school, had wanted to keep his precious baby daughter with him as much as possible. So Christie had been raised by a kindly nanny in a small house in the school grounds, spending long hours with her bookish yet devoted father. She had come to her aunt for the long summers. It was all she had ever known, and Christie gloried in it. She'd had two homes. Two people who adored her. She felt doubly blessed. And both of them had reassured her time and again that her mother had accepted the unplanned pregnancy joyously, despite knowing the risks her weak heart imposed, insisting that, if the worst happened, no great harm would be done. Her own life had taught her that it didn't matter who raised a child, as long as there was plenty of love. It was an abiding tenet of their lives. Christie's father believed it. Aunt Sassy certainly believed it. Christie had never once doubted it. And Lucas Merrick, when he was put to the test, had proved to believe it so passionately that he had begged Christie to have the child she was carrying adopted.

'It won't matter who raises it, Christie. As long as it has plenty of love,' he had said. His exact words.

She had been eighteen, and had not expected anything else from him at the time. She was pregnant, and full of the bravado of the young and inexperienced, but underneath her valiant exterior she had been frightened to death by what she had done.

The charred logs settled loosely in the grate. Christie pushed her shoulder-length hair back from her heart-shaped face and reached into the basket for fresh wood. The afternoon had drifted away and it was too late now to sort out the car. She would leave as early as possible in the morning. There was nothing to keep her in this place. She was sure of that now. Certainly not Lucas. No, not him. She wasn't fooled by that kiss. She knew exactly what he had felt—what he had been looking for.

Oh, *Lucas*. Would she never learn to forget? She had started to fall in love with him when she was four years old. The Merricks owned a great deal of the land around the village. They kept horses. Christie had loved horses in her babyish way. She remembered her aunt flagging down Lucas one day as he had cantered across the fields.

'Come over here, young man!' she had bellowed. 'You come here and let our Christabel pat that animal on the nose. She's got horses on the brain at the moment, she has.'

And while the scornful boy had none the less done as he was bid, Aunt Sassy had gathered Christie into her arms so that she could reach across the gate and stroke the horse's nose. She remembered even now looking up to smile her gratitude to the generous rider, and being startled for the first time by the brilliance of those alert, questioning eyes. Extraordinary auburn eyes, set deep in a sun-burned face, shadowed by floppy dark hair. Christie sighed wistfully, then got to her feet and stretched. All this remembering wasn't doing her any good at all.

The house, luckily, contained everything she needed to sustain life until morning. The electricity had been cut off, but the cooker ran on bottled gas and there were hurricane lamps and matches. There was even a store of tinned food, and tea and powdered milk. Her aunt hadn't known when she was taken into hospital with a painful flare-up of her condition that she would never return to her home. She had left everything in apple-pie order—waiting.

She made up the bed in the narrow room which had always been hers, and warmed up some soup which she ate, sitting beside the fire, while the evening sunshine streamed in through the window. She forced her eyes to avoid the photos of Sarah on the piano. The house seemed very empty since Lucas had left, and she didn't want to remind herself of how much she was missing her little daughter. The little child was everything to her these days. She had been worth every agonising moment. Giving up her foolish dreams that Lucas might one day come to love her had been a very small price to pay. Because they had only ever been dreams, anyway. Puerile dreams. Pointless dreams. Calf-love, they called it. And, in her case, hopelessly one-sided.

Lucas. She couldn't get him out of her mind. In London she could banish him for days at a time, but here, especially after today, his face swam in front of her eyes unendingly.

She would go to bed early and bury him in sleep. She quickly found night things and towels of her aunt's. But when she went into the small bathroom and turned on the tap, only cold water gushed out. And when she looked down at her feet, still streaked with mud, she realised that she needed a bath more badly than she had done since that summer when she and Ellen had decided to build a dam and Lucas had found her sitting in the mud and had let her ride home behind him, her arms around his waist, while the horse had walked sedately back to the cottage...

Oh, damn it. It was going to crack her up, remembering like this. She needed something to occupy her mind every bit as much as she needed a bath... Which was when she remembered the old tin bath in the outhouse. Oh, excellent! It would serve both purposes admirably.

A great deal of clattering and crashing was involved in the procedure, and a great many saucepans and a great deal of calor gas. But at last she was indulging a memory which had nothing whatsoever to do with Lucas Merrick. She was bathing in front of the fire, just as she had done when she was a small child, before the bathroom had been installed. The soap was in a saucer beside her. The fire roared away, throwing out a generous heat. Her hair was tied up in a ponytail to keep it dry, just as she used to wear it then. The only difference was that the figure who came unexpectedly into the room wasn't her aunt this time, but Lucas Merrick.

CHAPTER TWO

CHRISTIE was absolutely speechless. The heat of the fire seemed suddenly to increase. Propelled by modesty, her hands flew to cover her breasts, but they were quite inadequate to the purpose. All of her things were still in the car—she didn't even have a flannel to drape over herself. 'Lucas!' she hissed furiously.

Lucas took a few steps further into the room, then stood still. His eyes came to rest on her with that same cold severity. 'Is this intentional—this...this display?' he asked tersely.

'Don't be so stupid,' she returned angrily. 'How could it be? The immersion heater isn't working. The electricity is off. How on earth could I have planned something like this?' She hugged her arms tighter around her breasts.

He shrugged. 'Point taken,' he said at last, but the note of disdain was still very much there.

'Good grief, Lucas!' she exclaimed sharply, her tongue governed by a sudden bitter impulse. 'You've really changed, you know? You're every bit as unpleasant as the suggestion you just made. Now get out of here. I find the idea of a man like...like *you* looking at me extremely disturbing.'

'So you liked it when I looked at you that other time, eh, Christie?'

'I didn't say that.'

His shoulders hunched dismissively. 'Didn't you? It scarcely matters. I can remember exactly how much you enjoyed it, anyhow. I don't need you to confirm it. Or deny it, come to that... Though if you're planning to deny it, don't bother. I shan't believe you.'

Was she mistaken or was there something of that old scathing humour dancing around the edges of his words? Christie's skin flamed afresh as she remembered how she'd been with him that night. Her fingers started to shake, and she had to bite down on her lip to still the quivering.

'You're embarrassed...' he observed slowly, his voice softening. The unyielding tautness which had controlled both his voice and his posture seemed to be seeping away...

'Of course I am,' she hissed shakily.

'How round your eyes grow when you're embarrassed, Christie. Like pretty blue saucers. You looked at me that way when I found you down by the stream with your dress tucked in your drawers, plastered in mud...'

'I was eleven years old. Eleven-year-old girls don't like to be teased.'

'*You* never minded being teased, Christie.' He was teasing her now.

She glowered at him. She had never minded Lucas teasing her, it was true. Any attention from his quarter had been welcome, after all. 'I did...' she insisted vehemently.

'You were embarrassed because your drawers were on show.'

Her scowl darkened. Well, of course she had been! What self-respecting eleven-year-old in her right mind would relish being discovered by her heart-throb building a dam, with her dress tucked in her knickers and mud all over her legs? 'Is that so surprising?' she muttered fiercely.

'All this modesty... All this embarrassment... How on earth does it fit into the picture, Christie?' he murmured sceptically. 'It may be all of a piece with the little girl who came to help out with our ponies. But it doesn't tally with the image you've created for yourself since, does it?'

She was more than just embarrassed now. She was totally unnerved by the way he seemed to be mutating in front of her eyes. That coldness had fled. In his dark eyes a warm light flickered. Taunting, mocking, but undeniably *warm*. He was back. The old Lucas—*her Lucas*—he was back.

'Image?' she protested uncertainly. 'How can I be responsible for the image you have of me? I haven't been back here for years. And you didn't know anything about me even then.'

'Didn't I?' he said quizzically.

'No. Of course not. At least... Well, of course you did a bit... I mean...' She screwed her eyes closed, then opened them very wide. 'Oh, this is stupid!' she insisted angrily. 'Why am I allowing myself to get dragged into this conversation? Go away, Lucas.'

'It's a good job,' he said tauntingly, 'that you didn't go in for the teaching profession, Christie. You'd have been hopeless. The kids would have torn you to shreds.'

'Oh, no, they wouldn't,' she returned hotly. 'You've made the mistake of using yourself as you used to be as the yardstick. Every class has one trouble-maker. If I'd been your teacher I'd have chucked you out.'

'But I wouldn't have gone, Christie... Don't you see?'

'*Lucas*! Go away.'

His jaw tilted, and she could see clearly the bump in his cheek where his tongue had come to lodge. A positively wicked smile captured his features, and his eyes shone with mirth. 'Oh, dear,' he murmured, and she could tell that he wanted to laugh.

'Really, Lucas...' she growled, closing her eyes again.

And then he did laugh, that rich, melodious laugh which, once it started, seemed to go on forever.

'I don't know what you find so funny,' she muttered. 'If you were a gentleman you'd never have come in here without knocking. And you certainly wouldn't be standing there and laughing at me.'

Lucas managed to quell his mirth at last. 'The trouble is,' he said drily, 'I came here to apologise for that kiss. Only now that I'm here I don't feel like apologising at all. In fact I very much want to kiss you again.'

Christie hunched forward and brought up her knees to preserve what shreds of modesty she had left. Resting her chin on her knees, and hugging them tight against her full, rounded breasts, she turned her head on one side to glower at him over her shoulder.

'I really do think you should leave, Lucas,' she said stiffly. 'Go on. Go away.'

He didn't. Now that he had stopped laughing his eyes no longer glittered humorously. They had darkened and looked almost hungrily at her. 'Do you mean that, Christie? Do you really want me to go...?'

She swallowed hard. 'Yes,' she insisted, but her voice was tiny, priggish—and not very convincing.

He didn't say anything in reply, and, frightened of the silence, she exclaimed, 'What on earth makes you think you have the right to come in and out of here without knocking, anyhow?'

'I didn't know I needed to knock to go out.'

'You know what I mean!' She sounded almost tearful with exasperation.

'You left your keys in the ignition of your car—which, incidentally, has embedded itself in some mud. There were a few keys on the ring—including the one for the front door. I know because it matches mine. Anyway, I decided to drop them in to you, but when I got here there weren't any lights showing, and I figured you'd probably gone back to the car, and would believe yourself locked out when you realised the keys had gone missing. I was going to leave them on the table, put the door on the latch, and go looking for you.'

Christie sighed haughtily. 'I thought you said you'd come here to apologise?'

'That too. Yes... Though I certainly shan't bother now.'

'Oh?'

'As I'm hoping to repeat the experience, I don't want to set a precedent... I wouldn't want to waste too much time saying sorry... Not for every little kiss...'

'Lucas! Will you go, please?'

He moved a little closer. 'Let me soap your back,' he said softly, and his voice was thicker now.

'Lucas!' she wailed, looking into his eyes. 'No!'

It was extraordinary. This Lucas, this wry, irreverent Lucas, breaking all the rules, was the very man she had loved. This was the man she had wanted so badly that she had deliberately set out to seduce him. No, she corrected herself. It hadn't been deliberate. She had acted entirely on instinct. She might have seduced him quite wantonly—known in advance that that was what she was going to do. But her actions had been beyond reason— beyond the control of her intense, fluid teenage emotions. Her life had lurched out of control quite horrifyingly that summer. Her feelings for Lucas had been the only certainty.

When he had tried to kiss her earlier she had resisted him. Despite her powerful physical response she had managed to turn away from him because, in essence, he hadn't seemed to be the same Lucas that she had always loved. Now that man was back with a vengeance, and with horror Christie realised that nothing had changed. She might be sitting in the bath, primly hugging her knees and mouthing platitudes of outrage, but, from somewhere deep inside, her love was crying out to him. She was aroused by his presence, aroused by the light in his eyes, by the knowledge that he wanted her. Shockingly, she wanted to stand up and walk across the room right into his arms. She wanted to let him kiss her and then kiss her again and again, and for him never, ever to be sorry for having done it. She wanted him to make love to her.

When they had made love that other time she had courted him quite flagrantly, believing that as things stood she had nothing at all to lose. She had loved him with all her heart. She had wanted him more than all the world. Just one time, she had told herself bravely, and I shall live uncomplainingly with the consequences for the rest of my life. And, loyal always to that impulse, that was exactly what she had done. She had known then, just as she knew now, that there was no future for her in loving Lucas. Her love would never be returned—would never conform to the happy-ever-after stereotype of her adolescent dreams. But at least she had had the memory of that night to hold on to, sustaining her, feeding her, as she had come to terms with the difficult aftermath of her decision.

Now, she found herself thinking, she still had nothing to lose. She still wanted him more than anything in the world. She was even now having to fight an almost overwhelming urge to relax her muscles, to stretch out in the bath, and then slowly to stand up and walk across to him. Oh, dear. A terrible craven weakness assailed her every time she looked in his direction. She loved him. She wanted him. She yearned to spread her hands across the slope of his broad shoulders, to lean against his tall, muscular frame. And to let him kiss her.

'If you want me to go, I shall...' he said huskily, but the corner of his mouth puckered, and she knew that he already understood how she felt. 'I went earlier. You didn't want me here then... It's different now, though, isn't it? We're different all of a sudden. Both of us...'

There was a shimmering pause—a little silence—and then his voice came again, soft and beguiling. 'Christie...?'

She couldn't speak. She could hardly breathe.

'I've never forgotten that night, Christie,' he said quietly, and he could have been speaking her own words.

She flashed him a looked of near-panic. 'Please' her eyes begged, and yet she didn't honestly know whether she was pleading with him to go or to stay.

Slowly he came nearer and crouched down beside her, his eyes reflecting the fierce red glow of the fire in their dark mirrors. His shirt-sleeves were rolled back, revealing the solid muscularity of his forearms. One hand reached out for the soap and took it from the saucer. Then he dipped the soap in the water and began to rub it across her hunched shoulder-blades. The soap was cupped in the palm of his big hand. She felt it slip across the surface of her skin, the heel of his hand leading the way, the tips of his fingers following.

'Oh, Lucas, no...' she gasped, cupping her bowed face in her hands.

'Why do you say that, Christie?' he whispered. 'Why do you say no?'

She shook her head slowly. 'I don't know...' she breathed, and a shiver ran up her spine as his fingertips kept up the figure-of-eight motion, feather-light, sliding easily over her skin in the pathway of the soap.

Looking determinedly away, a photo of Sarah as a baby caught her eye. She froze, staring at it, while his fingers trickled tantalisingly across her back. That, she told herself, should make you call a halt. Think of Sarah.

Since Sarah's birth she had never so much as been out with another man. Her child was beloved. Little Sarah needed nothing more. She certainly didn't need Christie to go in search of a substitute father for her. But ironically the sight of Sarah's round blue eyes had quite the reverse effect on Christie. Because Lucas was no substitute. This was the only man Christie would ever love. One day Sarah would ask why there wasn't a daddy in their home. One day Christie would have to tell her daughter the truth. Sarah had no father because Christie hadn't been able to accept second-best. Would Sarah thank her for not giving to Lucas what little she had to give, for not taking what little he wanted her to take? Lucas hadn't asked the question, after all. Lucas didn't want to know. Christie couldn't fool herself that making love with him would make one jot of difference to her child now. Sarah's sacrifice had already been made.

She took her hands away from her face and turned to look hard into Lucas's eyes. 'I'll get a rash if you rub any more of that soap on to my back,' she said, her voice dry and shaking.

He froze, his eyes questioning.

'Could you...?' She ran her tongue over her lips. 'Could you wash my feet instead?'

Lucas's response was to set down the soap, and scoop a little water over her shoulders with one big hand. And then he leant forward and let his lips brush across her nape, side to side, his lips slightly parted. She felt them nibble softly at her skin. The sensation was magical. It released all her confused thoughts—sending them shooting downwards into some black, fathomless well. As her mind emptied, so her senses roared into life to fill the vacuum. A heavy languor took hold of her limbs. Hot with desire, she unfolded her legs and straightened them out, pointing her toes, letting her fingers float on the surface of the warm water. His chin was grazing her spine as he planted tiny kisses down her back.

He moved to the foot of the tub, smiling lopsidedly. He squatted there on his hunkers, immobile, waiting and watching. Under his scrutiny her nipples, already flushed and swollen with anticipation, hardened into firm buds. Her neck arched, and her head dropped backwards a little, inviting his pleasure. His half-closed eyes opened fractionally wider, and the tip of his tongue appeared between his lips.

'You've changed,' he murmured. 'Your breasts... They were so small. Pink and white. Apple-blossom-fresh.'

Christie bit down on her full lower lip. Child-bearing had matured her figure, so that, although she was still small-waisted, her breasts were now full and round, her nipples dark and prominent. Her hips were more generously curved, more womanly, less boyish.

Last time when she had revealed herself to him he had ground out that she was the most beautiful creature he had ever set eyes upon. She had been a slender girl. Pink and white. Apple-blossom-fresh. Would he still want her now?

Ah, but he did. There could be no doubt. He grasped her ankles with a sudden ferocity, and ran his broad, strong hands up her wet calves. 'My God, Christie,' he said, his voice clotted with desire, 'Oh, my God, you are beautiful.' And his fingers bit into her flesh. With a rapid, rapacious movement his mouth came down and closed over one toe after another. His breath was hot, the movement of his lips almost fierce, as his teeth dragged lightly over each toe in turn. And then he came and lifted her bodily, dripping wet, swinging her up into his arms, and holding her as if she were no weight at all. And then he began to kiss her mouth.

Christie lost herself in that kiss. Her eyes closed, and desire clouded her blood, so that it seemed to stand quite still in her veins, making her skin hum with sensuality. Even the damp cotton of his shirt against her cheek heightened her arousal. It smelt of him. Faintly musky; warm. A male smell. His mouth was hard and demanding, moving swiftly and passionately against her own. She opened to him, letting his tongue enter her mouth, responding with her own furious urgency as tongue met tongue and teeth clashed in the hunger of their embrace.

Slowly he sank to his knees, cradling her on his lap, still kissing her. One hand reached out and took a towel from the floor, and then, towel in hand, he straightened up and took her in his arms up the narrow, creaking staircase. Christie closed her eyes as they went, breathing deeply, aware of his mouth hovering over hers, feeling his hot breath on her skin, sensing his tongue darting tantalisingly close to her own bruised lips.

Whether by chance or instinct, he made straight for the narrow room in which she had dreamed of him so many times. The bed was high—an Edwardian wrought-iron bedstead, broader than a modern single bed, narrower than a double. A bed made for the urgency of calf-love—not the relaxed comfort of a married embrace. The room faced west, and the evening light which spilled through the window was flushed and rosy. He laid her in the centre on top of the coverlet, stained pink with sunlight, and then he knelt over her, straddling her thighs. He took the towel in both hands and dried her breasts.

The towel was thin and rough. He laid it flat across her breasts, and then spread his palms over the sensitive mounds. Very gently, round and round, he moved his hands, taunting her proud nipples, teasing them into increasing awareness until they burgeoned hard and demanding against his flattened palms. Christie's head was propped on a pair of soft pillows. She watched his dark eyes become darker still, half hooded, as his own arousal consumed him. She witnessed the tautening of denim as his male need surged against the unyielding cloth. In her mind there existed nothing but this moment. She was only conscious of Lucas, here with her, caressing her, hauling her senses from their frozen past into a gloriously awakened present. Her lips were parted, her breathing tremulous as it followed the course of her pleasure. The roused peaks of her breasts throbbed with excitement, tugging hard on the thread which bound them to that dark inner centre, making it ache with the sweet pangs of its own need.

Then, with his fingers curled, he dragged the rough cloth down so that her full, flushed breasts were revealed. She arched her back as the towel freed her breasts into the cool air. Every inch of her craved him. Even a moment's loss of contact, loss of the pressure of his flesh on hers was like an open wound. He moved the towel to her stomach, gently patting dry her moist skin. By now Christie was almost ready to cry out the insistence of her need for him. She reached out her hands to his shirt-sleeves and grasped them, tugging him towards her. Beneath the soft cloth she felt muscle, hard as a rock, and that recognition of the power of his body sent further waves of desire sweeping mercilessly through her.

He came down upon her, his lips slightly parted, the tip of his tongue caught delicately between his teeth, and began to kiss her again. While mouth plundered mouth, her naked flesh sang out for him. The rough denim of his jeans was coarse against her skin, the soft cotton of his shirt caressing, the pressure of his maleness insistently demanding. Her fingers splayed against his back, hugging him close, relishing the packed layers of muscle manifest through the cloth. Her hand came around and squeezed between them, slipping inside the open collar of his shirt to touch his skin. The action seemed to inflame him. He raised his mouth from hers and took his weight on one elbow, the other hand tearing at the buttons of his shirt, yanking it free from the waistband of his jeans. And then his hands were in her hair, unknotting it, riffling through it, tumbling it around her warm cheeks, while his mouth met hers again. Now she felt the hair-roughened skin of his chest crushing against her breasts. She began to writhe and arch beneath him, alive with an urgent desire, unable to control the frantic necessity of her movements. He dragged his mouth down, tasting her neck, her shoulders, until his lips found her nipple and drew it deep into his mouth. Sucking hard on the nub of roused flesh, he sent her senses winging so close to the precipice that she tossed her head violently to one side and cried huskily, 'No, Lucas, please... Oh... yes... No...'

He drew back; then once again he knelt above her while he threw off his shirt and unzipped the taut fabric of his jeans. Slowly he revealed himself to her: broad, sloping shoulders; powerful arms; the hollow planes of his belly and flanks, sun-browned and hair-roughened. The dark hairs of his body shone in the dimming red light of sunset. And at the parting of his hard, solid thighs she saw at last the dark shadow of his desire, infinitely desirable, marking its course to the moist centre of her being. Hovering above her, his weight carried on his corded arms, he dipped his head again to the fullness of her breasts, letting his tongue dart to her nipples, plucking them between firm lips, dragging his teeth against their erect peaks until she raised her hips in a surge of such desperate craving that he moved his barbed chin to her cheek, and sent bone crushing against bone with the first powerful thrust.

She cried out as he entered her, the tightness of her moist flesh seeming at last to ease as he thrust again and again. Lucas was inside her. He was there again in that deep, dark place which would only ever be his. They were melded together, moving together, closing on that moment when they would be completely one. Tears of joy spilled on to her cheeks as his raucous cry rent the air with its ecstasy. She tumbled blindly with him, mindless now in the midst of her thundering pleasure, wave upon wave of blissful release rocking her flesh.

The still aftermath was another form of ecstasy. Satiated, buried beneath the sweet weight of his body, spent and draped across hers, her mind swam in and out of consciousness, as sleep beckoned. She could taste his sweat on her lips. Every breath she took was redolent of him and his satisfied desire. She felt the hair of his body tickling her skin, felt the silken expanse of his back beneath her heavy palms. And then she would feel nothing as sleep claimed her for a few moments, before freeing her back into the heady world of satisfied sensation. It was dark now, dark and warm, a safe heaven, buried beneath Lucas.

At last she felt him stir.

'I'm cold,' he groaned into her hair.

'Liar,' she whispered, running her hands over his warm shoulders.

He clenched his fingers against her and laughed softly. 'You think you know everything. But you're wrong.'

'I have evidence, Lucas. My hands are actually on your skin. It's warm.'

He shook his head. 'Lower,' he instructed, and she could picture the smile which would be teasing his lips as he said it. 'Move your hands lower.'

Her hands travelled down over the small of his back to the curve of his buttocks. 'Your bottom's cold,' she giggled.

Heavily he rolled to the outside edge of the bed, and with a great deal of uncomfortable shuffling he worked the bedclothes free and covered himself.

'Now *I'm* cold!' whispered Christie, in mock-complaint.

'Then,' he said in a low growl, 'you know what you can do about it.'

Tucked under the covers with him, she relished the physical warmth of his body as it curled around hers. And then she felt that other heat beginning to stir again, more gently this time, but no less insistently. In the dark, held close against his big frame, she allowed his tender fingers to light once again the fires of her sexual desire. Their coupling was slow and languorous, his lovemaking infinitely gentle, but the final satisfaction was no less fierce for all that. When finally she slept, her back to him, his body curved around hers, his arm resting in the hollow of her waist, the pad of his thumb nestling in her navel, she felt utterly complete and utterly happy.

A little after dawn he stroked her hair and kissed her flushed cheeks. 'I'll be back,' he murmured, and she smiled contentedly, nodding mildly, barely awake. It was nearly nine before she wakened properly. The sky beyond the window was blue and white, and the treetops visible from her prone position shook in a stiff breeze. A huge smile broke on her lips as she remembered. Lucas. He'd be back. They had made love, and he'd wanted her. Some time during the course of the day she would have to face up to her actions—but for now she would just snuggle down under the bedclothes and be happy. She could allow herself that much, at least.

She went on being happy for a long time. When she sat up and looked down at her nakedness she felt particularly happy, because it reminded her that Lucas had wanted her. And then, very abruptly and very sharply, she stopped feeling happy and started feeling ashamed. Slowly her skin began to flush a horrible dull red. Because she had been fooling herself. Oh, Lucas *had* desired her—but he had only wanted her in a carnal sense. She'd known that all along, of course, but she hadn't thought it through... If she'd only had herself to think of she might have persuaded herself that it was enough. But there was Sarah to think of too.

Little Sarah whom he didn't want to know. She clapped her hands over her face and clenched her teeth. She'd convinced herself last night that this couldn't hurt Sarah, but she was wrong. She had been so certain that if ever she met him again he would at least ask, and, though she hadn't known what she would say, the conviction that he would want to know had sustained her. But he hadn't asked, and now she had to face up to the fact that he never would, and one day she was going to have to answer all Sarah's questions as honestly as she could—all by herself. How would she explain this one night? Perhaps it wouldn't be so difficult... But Lucas had said that he would be back. And he would only come back for one thing... So how would Sarah feel about other nights, other meetings, when she was old enough to understand? Christie groaned desperately. She mustn't see Lucas again. She must never let herself be tempted again as she had been last night. There could be no excuses now as there had been that first time.

She wasn't a teenager any more. She was an unmarried mother with a child of four. She had a good job, which supported them both quite nicely, and a flat in a shabby but respectable part of the city. And she had just spent the night with Lucas, who despised her. Lucas, who must surely be thinking that she was an experienced woman now, who did that kind of thing regularly. After all, that was exactly what she had intended him to think when she had made love with him the very first time. She hadn't exactly behaved like a blushing virgin on either occasion. She had thought that making love with him again would be no more than a simple balm to the endless ache of loving him. But now it felt like a knife turned in an open wound, stirring a pain so sharp that the tears just couldn't be stemmed.

CHAPTER THREE

CHRISTIE'S head was still buried in the pillow, her face wet with tears, when Lucas returned. She felt the weight of him bow the bedsprings as he sat down. Then his hand came to rest on the curve of her hip. Its warmth penetrated through the bedclothes.

'Christie?'

'Go away,' she mumbled into the pillow.

'Come on, Christie...' His voice was cajoling, his hand mobile as it rubbed at the prominence of her hip-bone.

She turned her face towards the wall, desperate that he shouldn't know that she'd been crying—or why, come to that. If he realised how upset she was, he might start to probe. Quite honestly she didn't know if she was clever enough to fend off too many prying questions. All she knew was that she mustn't on any account let him discover how special last night had been for her. It might impel him to ask the very question he wouldn't put to her voluntarily. If he didn't *want* to know, then she wouldn't on any account force the information on him. It would be too humiliating to bear.

Bleakly she acknowledged that she had to finish matters with Lucas now, once and for all. For Sarah's sake. But it made her ache with a grief so terrible that she could hardly bear it. Everything else that she had ever done for her child's sake had been easy. Giving birth, existing for months on end with no sleep, being frightened to death and yet not showing it when her child was ill; those gifts had been given so readily. But this was different. Lucas wanted her at last after all these years, and she was turning him away.

'Honestly, Lucas,' she sighed dully, 'I would much rather you went. Last night was a big mistake. Let's just leave it at that.'

His hand travelled down over her hip and across her thigh until it lay on the covers beside her, ceasing to rest on any part of her body. The gesture was slight, but even so it felt like a bereavement. His hand had been there, alive, touching her. Now it was not. Tears rushed to her eyes again, but, almost panic-stricken by the idea of his sensing her hurt, she furiously blinked them back.

'It didn't feel like a mistake to me,' he said coldly.

Christie nibbled on the end of one thumb. 'Well, it did to me,' she returned. 'Sorry, Lucas, but that's that.'

The bed creaked as Lucas stood up. She dared not turn her head to look.

'I had to go and see the horses. I had a trainer coming over to watch them first thing this morning. Surely you understood?'

She sniffed. It had been an inadvertent reflex—an attempt to keep the tears at bay. It sounded derisive.

'For God's sake, are you so much of a spoilt child that you can't comprehend that working with animals entails that kind of thing?' he snapped harshly.

Christie bit even harder on the end of her thumb. So he thought she was being petulant? That she resented his having to leave at dawn? A spoilt child... Lucas wouldn't like that. If there was one thing that Lucas didn't like, after all, it was children...

'Really...?' She dragged out the word insolently.

'You've obviously forgotten everything you ever learned from helping with the ponies.'

'The ponies? Oh, yeah...I'd forgotten.' She steeled herself. 'But I did that for fun—I used to like horses then. You employ people to do the work for you now, Lucas... You don't have to do anything you don't want to do, surely? You could have stayed.'

'I stayed as long as I could.' His voice was gratingly rough.

She gave a huffy shrug, hoping to strengthen the impression of childish pique. 'I was surprised you stayed so long, actually,' she said tartly. 'I'd have thought you would have gone back last night—after we'd...you know...made love.'

There was a long pause. She could sense tension beginning to build in the air, like a premonition of thunder.

'Don't your lovers usually stay the night, Christie?' he suddenly snapped, his attitude reeking of contempt.

She took a deep breath. 'Not usually, no,' she returned casually. 'After all, I have my daughter to consider...'

'Oh, yes. Your daughter.'

Christie shivered inwardly at the sour edge to his voice. Then, determined to press onwards, she shrugged again, very obviously this time, flouncing the bedclothes a little to make her point. 'However, she isn't with me, is she? Which means that for once I was able to look forward to the luxury of spending an entire night with my...well, "lover" was your word, wasn't it?' She sighed noisily. 'Naturally I was disappointed.'

The pause this time was so long that her heart started to pound. She was terrified he might hear.

'Nowhere near as near as disappointed as I am, Christie,' he said, and his voice was so contorted with disgust that she scarcely recognised it.

Then he said slowly, 'Look at me, Christie. Why don't you look at me?'

She made an irritated sucking noise with the tip of her tongue. 'Do I have to? I'm comfortable like this... I really don't want to turn over.'

She lay rigid, facing the wall, waiting for a response which never came. For a horrible moment she thought that he would strip back the bedclothes and turn her over and force her to meet his eye. But he didn't. Instead he confined his violence to slamming the bedroom door so hard that the window shivered in its frame. She didn't draw breath until she heard the final creak of the stairs, and the sullen bang of the front door.

She rolled over on her back and stared at the ceiling, her hands folded stiffly underneath her chin. Her mouth was quite dry. Her lips felt as if they would crack if she so much as moved them. But she was safe now. He had gone. She had made him think badly of her yet again. And of course it was better that way, because it stopped her hoping. It protected Sarah. And it was the only answer. She flung back the bedclothes and got up, quite desolate now as she began to assimilate it all. He had gone. And he hadn't wanted to know.

Obviously the last thing he wanted was to know for sure whether or not Sarah was his child. Well, she was Christie's child. The joy of her life. He had never wanted her to have the baby. He had urged her to give it up for adoption. Then, of course, he had thought it could not possibly be his. Now, at the very least, he must have his doubts. It wasn't as though things had been kept quiet. There had been a big announcement in the parish magazine for a start. Anybody who could count back from nine to zero would realise that the child had been conceived in the village. Everyone else would want to know. Everyone except Lucas, she thought bitterly.

And yet it was no good; despite everything, she couldn't bring herself to be sorry that they'd made love last night. Time had played a strange trick on them. It had turned them back into the people they had been that other summer. And anyway, she had been utterly powerless once he'd smiled that way.

She kept the tears at bay. She'd had plenty of practice, after all. Hard work. That was the answer. She glanced about her with a determined air. The windows. That was it... She'd clean the windows. Within minutes she was outside in the stiff May breeze, working the cream in to the corners of the small panes and then furiously polishing them clean.

She was so intent on what she was doing that she didn't hear the Range Rover pull up behind her. She didn't notice Lucas's arrival at all until he was right behind her. 'You're very industrious this morning...' he said, and, the way he said it, it didn't exactly sound like high praise.

'Yes,' she returned neutrally, hoping he wouldn't notice that she had almost jumped out of her skin.

Lucas rested one shoulder against the wall, and watched her. She jabbed the cloth into the corners, rubbing away the streaks of polish.

'Why are you cleaning the house? What's the point if it's to be cleared and sold?'

'I didn't say it was going to be sold. And anyway, why shouldn't I clean it? It needs it.'

'Christie, you have a child waiting for you back in London. A quick once-over with the duster I could understand—but polishing the windows? What's the matter with you? Don't you want to get back home to her?'

Christie stopped and glared at him. 'That was a really horrible thing to say, Lucas. Of course I do.'

He shrugged contemptuously.

Suddenly her control started to slide. 'Lucas, you've had a reputation for many things over the years. Stubbornness; wildness; ruthlessness, even. They've said all sorts of things about you—not that *you* ever cared. But the one thing I've never heard anyone complain of is your out-and-out nastiness. On the contrary. You've been credited with a good deal of charm. So why is it that I'm the only one who never gets charmed by you? Why am I privileged to know just how unkind you can be?'

Lucas just raised his eyebrows and gave a half-smile. She hastily turned back to her task. She shouldn't have said that. If she provoked a row now things might be said which were much, much better left unsaid.

Lucas had no such compunction. 'You haven't answered my question. Why are you cleaning the windows?'

'It's a lovely day,' she pointed out archly. 'The sun is shining—well, on and off. And the air down here is wonderful after London. I'm doing it for the sheer pleasure of it, if you must know.'

'What a curious combination of pastimes, Christie...' he said sardonically. 'Sex for the hell of it I can understand. But cleaning windows? How do the two fit together? They certainly don't match the picture of the cool young career woman—a single parent by choice.'

'I didn't plan my life that way, Lucas,' she returned, trying to keep the hurt out of her voice. 'OK—I chose it when the options narrowed, but I didn't set out to be what I am today. And anyway, I can't see any reason why the fact that I found last night's... encounter... physically gratifying should mean that I can't also enjoy being out in the fresh air, listening to the bird-song and shining up the windows.'

'Oh, please spare me, Christie! You make it all sound so wonderfully bucolic. So romantic, even... The age-old story of the earthy young milkmaid enjoying a tumble in the hay and then returning merrily to her work, as happy as the day is long...'

'You're twisting my words!'

'No, Christie. You're the one who's twisting things. Last night's "encounter" was anything but romantic, wasn't it? Oh, why the hell did you come here?'

She couldn't reply. She kept her lips pressed together into a hard, straight line and rubbed fiercely at the glass in front of her nose.

'So let's get to the bottom of it... The house *isn't* going to be sold. And your aunt won't be moving back. She's not fit enough. So who are you shining it up for? Is it going to be let?'

Still Christie didn't reply.

'Is it?'

'No.'

'Aaah... Christie! Then it's you, isn't it? You're moving back down here yourself?'

'I didn't say that,' she muttered guardedly.

'Then it *is* true?'

'Of course it isn't.'

'It must be. The way you denied it gave you away.'

'I'm not moving down here, and that's the truth.'

He narrowed his eyes and surveyed her. 'Now we're looking at the mathematician's brain...' he murmured. 'Strictly accurate, but... Let me see... You're not moving down here, but... but you're considering it? Yes, that's why you're here, isn't it?'

'Yes. All right. Yes. If you must know.'

'So what made you want to come back to this particular spot, Christie?'

'I don't. It wasn't even my idea.'

'Well, well... It could be rather interesting having you for a neighbour again. The villagers will be delighted as long as you keep your windows so clean. Though what they'll make of your—er—other source of pleasure will remain to be seen. I thought I was the only one to set tongues wagging around here. But it seems I might have to share the honour.'

'Oh, shut up, Lucas. Just shut up.'

Oddly enough he did. He looked at her, though, and it was much worse than being spoken to by him.

At last he asked curtly, 'Do you have your car keys on you?'

She scowled back at him. 'No. They're indoors. Why do you want them?'

'I need to let the handbrake off if I'm to tow it out of the mud.'

Christie's mouth tightened. She started to rub furiously at the window. 'It's all right. I can get someone else to do it.'

Lucas surveyed her coldly. 'I thought you *liked* letting me do you favours, Christabel?'

Anger flared in her blue eyes. 'That's a terrible...' She stopped herself. She was supposed to be hell-bent on making him think the worst of her, after all.

'Well, of course,' she said sarcastically. 'So I do. I'll go in and fetch them for you now. How neighbourly and thoughtful you've become in your dotage, Lucas...'

A reaction flickered deep in his eyes, but she didn't stop to assess it. No point. And anyway, she couldn't risk giving herself away by looking at him too lingeringly. Hurriedly she made her way into the house.

He waited for her outside. When she returned he gripped her arm and led her to the Range Rover. She prised his fingers off and shook herself free, rubbing at the cold imprint of his fingers on her flesh.

'You hurt me,' she complained.

'Really?' he returned, with evident satisfaction. Then, 'Get in,' he commanded, opening the passenger door of the Range Rover.

As soon as they were both inside he roared off, slewing the big vehicle around into the narrow rutted lane outside the house.

'Why do I have to come with you?' she asked bitterly.

'Good manners,' he snapped. 'It's your car I'm rescuing, after all. And to tell me exactly what you're planning to do. I'm sick of your evasions. Are you coming back here or not?'

Christie paused, wondering how much to tell him. The truth, she decided. Up to a point, anyway. 'I came down here to take a look at the house and consider the idea. At Aunt Sassy's insistence, you understand. But I have no intention of falling in with the plan.'

'Doesn't your aunt like having you and the child as neighbours?' It was back again. That fierce contempt.

'Of course she does!' exclaimed Christie furiously. 'She loves seeing so much of Sarah.'

'Then why does she want you to move over a hundred miles away?'

Christie suppressed a sigh. It was for Sarah's sake that her aunt was pressing her to move.

'It's not right for a child to be brought up in a flat like that in the middle of London,' she had announced. 'She needs fresh air and the freedom to run about. You had it. Why do you want to stop our Sarah from having it as well? There's a perfectly good house sitting empty there, while this child has to live like a battery chicken.'

'I take her to the park every day.'

But Aunt Sassy had only snorted the louder. 'Park!' she had exclaimed. 'Dirty old place full of goodness knows what. Blooming ducks on the pond look half soaked. You should go. You can do your computer work anywhere. You told me that yourself. As long as there's a telephone line, you said...'

'Well, Christie...?' Lucas's voice was dark with derision.

'She thinks Sarah would benefit from living in the country. That's all. But she doesn't relish the idea of us moving so far away, of course. In fact that's one of the major reasons why I won't be coming.'

'For your aunt's sake?'

'Yes. That's right.'

'How noble of you to put your aunt's needs before those of your child.'

'You're twisting my words again, Lucas.'

'Oh? So you don't agree that your daughter would be better off being raised in the country?'

'I... No, I don't. She's happy where she is.'

'And you are too, I take it.'

'Very.'

'So you like city life?'

'Yes.'

'You like traffic fumes and noise and big buildings.'

'I didn't say that.'

'No? Then what is it that you like so much about the city, Christie?'

Christie struggled to think of a suitably convincing reply, but Lucas didn't wait for her answer.

'Is it the anonymity that you like, Christie? The endless supply of men?'

'That's right,' she flashed back bitterly.

'And what does your daughter think of all these boyfriends?'

'I—er—I told you earlier. She doesn't get to meet them.'

'Really? Isn't that a rather selfish way of choosing a daddy for your little girl? You try them out in bed before you make the introductions?'

'I... It's important that anyone I—er—I mean Sarah won't be happy if I'm not, will she? Compatibility is...is important. When I meet someone with whom I'm compatible, then I'll introduce him to Sarah.'

'So you've never found a man yet who lives up to your expectations in bed sufficiently convincingly for you to take it a step further? Like a visit to the zoo?' There was a disdainful silence. 'Tell me, Christie... Do any of these studs even know that you have a child?'

'Oh, shut up, Lucas. Leave it alone for goodness' sake. It's none of your business how I choose to live my life.'

Lucas gave a harsh laugh. 'No. Indeed it isn't. Thank goodness. But I'm rather enjoying discovering how our sweet little stable-maid has turned out. It's very enlightening.'

'I don't live my life in order to provide you with entertainment.'

'That's exactly what you seemed to be doing last night.'

'Last night was a mistake, Lucas.'

'Was it? Yes. I can see that it must have been. Gossip spreads in the country. But don't worry—I shan't give anything away. For once I find I do mind what other people think. I wouldn't enjoy having my name linked with yours.'

Christie sat in stiff silence, unable to think of a response. It was important that she didn't protest too much. It was important that he thought she was an experienced woman, in control of her own life. She had *wanted* him to think badly of her, after all. But not this badly. It was unbearable.

'You didn't answer my question, Christie,' he said coldly, swinging the vehicle to a halt some yards in front of her own little car. He killed the engine, but made no move to get out.

'Which question?' she returned sullenly. 'There have been rather a lot.'

'Do your boyfriends even know that you have a child?'

'I... Of course. These are the 1990s, Lucas. My father and my aunts take a very modern attitude to my unmarried status.' Astonishingly modern, Christie had to concede. Their enthusiastic reception of her dismal news had taken the eighteen-year-old Christie entirely by surprise. 'You're the only one trapped in the Dark Ages, Lucas. No doubt you think the pair of us should be shunned by the world. Well, I'm pleased to be able to tell you that we're not. I'm proud of my daughter. Very proud. I don't make a secret of her existence to anyone.'

Anger was flaring inside her like a beacon. She was quite unable to contain herself when her feelings for her daughter were called into question.

Lucas let out a short, derisive laugh. 'But not proud enough of her to introduce her to your men-friends? To allow them to make up their own minds?'

'It's not like that!'

'Isn't it? I have to admit that I shop around for a good stud to offer to my brood mares—but the stallions don't exactly play a large role in raising the foals. If they did, I'd set about things differently.'

'I'm not a *horse*, Lucas!'

'No,' he agreed harshly. 'You're a sheep. Remember? A black sheep.'

'*Stop it*, Lucas.'

'Every now and then one of my mares will reject her foal. I find the best answer is to separate them.'

Christie looked at Lucas in panic. What on earth did he mean by that? Oh this was awful. She had gone way over the top in letting him believe that she was so wanton. What if he tried to have Sarah taken away from her? He couldn't possibly do it, of course... Unless he tried to prove... No. It was absurd... He couldn't, surely? Even so, she was frightened. Was he threatening her? Desperately she began back-pedalling...

'I'm a good mother, Lucas,' she protested urgently. 'I am... I really am.'

'Are you? How would anyone know? You live an anonymous life in the heart of a vast city.'

'Aunt Sassy knows. She thinks I am. And my father does.'

'Your aunt thinks the child would benefit from country living. Or perhaps she just thinks that it would be better for the child if you were cut off from your endless supply of studs. At any rate, she must have reservations of some sort or she wouldn't have suggested you move down here.'

'She... she just thinks that fresh air and freedom to run about are good for children. She loves Sarah. It's only natural that she should want the best for her.'

'And you don't?'

'Of course I do!'

'But you don't think that the country is a good place to raise a child?'

'All a child needs is love. That's all. Love.'

Lucas eyed her coldly. 'How do you know that? Was love enough for you? You had plenty of love. You also used to arrive here every summer looking pale and thin. And you'd be shy. Then you ran free for two months every year. Climbed trees. Rode our ponies. Paddled in the stream. Joined the gangs of local kids. Didn't that have any effect on you? Wasn't it good for you?'

Christie looked down at her hands knotted in her lap. That was how he remembered her. A pale, thin, shy child, paddling in streams, running wild with the gangs of local children. A child who donned make-up and women's clothes for a party one night, and threw herself at him, almost begging him to make love with her. A child who'd made a mess of her life. Who'd turned out badly, despite being loved. A child whom he despised.

'Lucas, you're assuming far too much. You know very little about me. My father and I didn't live in a city. I had plenty of fresh air at Braizeneath.'

'But very little freedom. It must have been a strange place for a little girl to grow up, in the grounds of a boys' school.'

'What are you suggesting? That I've run wild since I grew up?'

'That's pretty much the picture I get.'

Christie cupped her hands over her face and pinched the bridge of her nose between her two index fingers. What should she do? Should she let him go on believing that she was some kind of uncontrolled wanton—out every night of the week, drinking in nightclubs and meeting men? She gave an involuntary shudder at the thought. She had gone way too far...

'You've got things wrong,' she muttered.

'Have I? Isn't it the availability of men that's keeping you in London after all, Christie? Is it something else?'

'Yes. I don't have lots of boyfriends... I only said that because you were goading me. I just have... an ordinary sort of amount. I mean, occasionally I go out with someone... you know. Like any woman of my age would. But the reason I stay in London is because I... just like it there.'

His eyes narrowed. 'Is there one man in particular, Christie? That would explain a lot...'

'No. I told you that yesterday.'

He tilted back his head speculatively. 'You told me there wasn't a man important to you. That doesn't mean there's not a man important to your child...' He paused, then added, 'You're in contact with her father, aren't you, Christie? He sees her...? So *that's* why you don't muddy the waters by introducing your child to your other boyfriends.'

Christie's mouth fell open in surprise. She hadn't expected him to draw that conclusion. It was almost as if he were wilfully misconstruing the facts... She clapped her hand to her face to prevent the denial from coming too hastily to her lips. At least he'd modified his view of her now. There was that to be thankful for...

'I—er...' she stuttered anxiously. She closed her eyes. Why on earth had she come down here? Oh, this was dreadful... dreadful...

'You told me you didn't want to ruin his life. But if you were as fond of each other as you made out, it really didn't make sense.'

She struggled to pull herself together, to get a grip on what he was saying. Fond of each other? She hadn't said that, had she? Or at least, she hadn't meant by it what he thought she'd meant. She'd just said what she'd said in order to convince Lucas that the baby couldn't be his. James's name had been the only one which had sprung to mind—for reasons which at the time had seemed quite obvious—and which now, with hindsight, seemed utterly absurd. Oh, dear. Poor James. She hadn't thought of him for years.

'None of this is any of your damned business, Lucas,' she snapped, trying to cover her confusion with a display of irritation. 'Now if you're so determined to play the good neighbour, you can get that car of mine out of the mud. I'm going up to the shop to see Maudie.'

And with that Christie jumped out of the car and set off at a near-trot. She heard the driver's door bang and looked over her shoulder to check that he wasn't following her. He wasn't. He was leaning against the side of the Range Rover, his arms folded across his chest, his chin tilted as if to catch the sun. Even at this distance she fancied she caught the auburn glint of his eyes.

Oh, God. Poor James. She hadn't thought of him for years. She had been about to leave school when it happened. She had been an adult. Not that Lucas would notice. He had still teased her and treated her as the child she had always been in his eyes. In a matter of weeks she'd be going to spend her last summer with him in Gloucestershire. After that she would start her training course, and then begin work. The long summer holidays, rising early to exercise the old ponies while Lucas tended the hunters, would be at an end forever.

One Saturday she bought clothes and make-up in anticipation of seeing him again, and showed them off to her father, who murmured his approbation. But her father's opinion didn't satisfy her. He was old and out of touch. She wandered over to the school house, where the older boys boarded. In recent years the school had been taking a handful of day-girls into the sixth form. Christie had been one of them, so these youths were no strangers to her. Her appearance in their day-room raised a raucous cheer and a chorus of wolf-whistles, not to mention a few rather crude schoolboyish remarks.

Christie pulled a face at the assembled crew, regretting her decision to seek out their collective opinion. But on her way out James Lakey, a rather shy boy who blushed easily, braved the jeers of his classmates to follow her.

'Take no notice of them, Christie,' he said, turning red in the face. 'They've all got a crush on you, you know? That's what makes them behave so badly.'

When he stutteringly offered to take her out she accepted, impressed by his thoughtfulness, and anxious to protect him from the taunts of his classmates. He even offered to change out of his tracksuit and take her somewhere special where she could show off her dress to advantage, but she dragged him off swiftly, eager to get away from the crowd in the common-room. They ended up at a folk club. James stuttered a little, and blushed so furiously all evening that she felt quite sorry for him. He really was an awfully nice boy. Unfortunately his shyness was catching. Whenever his conversation ran dry he frowned and sucked his upper lip down under his lower one as if he were concentrating very hard on some world-shattering problem. Christie found, to her horror, that as the evening progressed she began to imitate him. She hoped that no one was watching. They must look like a pair of chimpanzees, sitting there silently, sucking their upper lips.

On the walk back James began to cough rather theatrically. It worried Christie. Each time he coughed he raised his hand to his mouth. On the third occasion he brought his arm down in a sweeping arc so that it landed heavily on her shoulder. He left it there. Oh, dear. If only it could have been Lucas at her side, walking with her beside the river in the moonlight, she would have been in seventh heaven. As it was she was squirming with embarrassment.

When they reached the municipal bench overlooking the bend in the river James claimed to have tired legs and requested a halt. Well, what could she say? For all she knew it might even be true... Except, of course, that she knew it wasn't. And then, just as she had suspected it might, it began.

He loomed over her and pressed his mouth to hers. Christie screwed her eyes tight shut. Oh, dear; oh, dear. This was awful. Of course, it was very kind and thoughtful of James to want to kiss her, and he'd obviously had such a struggle to pluck up the courage that she could hardly push him away, but it was obvious that he knew no more about kissing than she did. Even so, she was quite sure he shouldn't be pressing his face quite so close to hers, because her lips hurt where they were squashed against her teeth.

Their noses clashed. James swivelled his head a little so that his downy cheek was close against her nostrils. How on earth were you supposed to breathe? She tilted her head back as far as it would go, which cleared her airway a little, but meant that she made a strange clicking noise when she swallowed. She didn't think that was supposed to happen, either... Oh, help! This was dreadful. James changed position, and suddenly she couldn't breathe again. She leaned a little further back. James's hands lay leadenly on her shoulders. He increased the pressure of mouth against mouth one more time. Little by little the inexperienced pair keeled helplessly over to one side, until Christie was pinned uncomfortably against the seat of the municipal bench, the top half of her body lying down while her legs still attempted to sit. James's body was draped in an ungainly fashion across her own as their mouths continued to try to do what, Christie couldn't help feeling, should have come just a little more naturally.

At last James gave up. He sat up abruptly and sucked hard on his upper lip. Christie leapt thankfully to her feet and straightened her rumpled dress. She gazed helplessly at him for a moment. Poor James. He was such a kind boy and he looked so mournful...

'I'm sorry...' He sighed.

'Er—that was very nice, James...' she lied encouragingly.

His face seemed to brighten a little in the moonlight. 'Was it...?' he asked eagerly.

She nodded, and then, before he could attempt a repeat performance, she added, 'Come on, Lakey... Race you back... Last one to the school gate's a hairy mammoth...'

James's legs had obviously benefited from the rest. He won the race in style.

CHAPTER FOUR

HALF WAY back from the shop Christie stopped and admonished herself. She was dragging her heels, her stomach was in knots, and she was behaving like a fugitive. She had to act as if she could handle Lucas, no matter how unpleasant he was. On no account must she let him guess that he had the power to disturb her. If he realised that, he might begin to realise an awful lot of other things too, and, dammit, she wasn't about to let that happen. She picked up her heels and began to march confidently back to her car. If he didn't have the decency to ask, she was damned if she'd help him guess. Anyway, it wasn't even as if she wanted him to know. She'd made a vow and she'd honour it, come what may.

Lucas was sitting at the wheel of his vehicle, the door open, and one long leg dangling out. His arms were folded across his chest. He looked bored. Her little car was safely out of the mud at the side of the road.

'Thanks, Lucas,' she said crisply.

His eyes surveyed her coldly. He didn't say anything.

'I...I guess I'll be off, then,' she added a little less confidently, making her way towards her own car.

'Yes. I don't suppose I shall see you again, Christie.'

Did he sound pleased at the prospect? Hard to tell. His voice had been curiously toneless.

'Er—no. Thanks for the fire and the tow and—er—everything.'

'You mean for last night?'

Ouch. His voice wasn't neutral now. It was acid enough to burn.

'Last night was a mistake, Lucas.'

He started his engine, and leaned out to close the door. 'So you keep saying. And I can take it you *won't* be moving back down here, then?'

'No. I won't.'

He gave her a long, assessing look. 'Then we won't be tempted to make the same mistake for the third time, will we, Christie?' His eyebrows curved upwards disparagingly.

'No.' She sounded so calm. It was extraordinary. She wanted to choke, to scream, to kick and punch and wail. Instead all that happened was that she made one neat, clipped, polite little word with her blanched lips and her dry tongue.

His head tilted backwards. 'Not that there'd be any temptation now, Christie. You can rest assured of that. Feel free to change your mind about moving down here. I shan't come round to—er—to warm up the *house* for you again.'

'Oh...yes...right...' She was inside her own car now, her head bent over the dashboard, her hand fumbling shakily for the keys in the ignition. The key turned; the engine growled. She even used the indicators to let him know—oh, so politely—that she was pulling out from behind the bulk of his immobile car; out of the shimmering slipstream of his exhaust; out of his life.

Sarah was delighted to see her mum again. Back in their flat Christie cuddled the child on her knee, smelling the sweetness of her skin and burying her face in her hair. At night Christie cried, just as she had done during those months after the birth when she had waited for Lucas to contact her and ask, 'When exactly was she born?' But May melted into June and then July into August, just as it had done then.

In August it got hot. Christie took Sarah to the park. The ducks looked shabby. The settled spell brought the smell of pitch sweating out of the roadways. Sarah got a summer cold. Sarah's cold developed into a barking cough. Christie carried her in her arms to the surgery. She looked at the child as they sat in the waiting-room. Sarah looked pale despite all those visits to the park. Nice Dr Hughes smiled reassuringly and said there was a lot of it about, and that all children got coughs, and you only had to worry if... Well, Sarah's was a perfectly ordinary cough. Not a worrying cough. Not croup or asthma or bronchitis. Just ordinary. Just the sort of cough that there was a lot of about in town this summer.

Christie told Aunt Sassy what the doctor had said. Aunt Sassy looked at Christie the same way she used to look at Christie when she put the tea-leaves down the sink, instead of carrying them out to the drain in the back. 'Those pipes'll get blocked if you don't watch out,' she used to say. 'Maybe not today, but one day.'

This time her aunt didn't need to say anything; Sarah's pale face said it all. Christie spent nearly a week making the arrangements. When she got off the M5 near Dursley she opened the car window to let in the fresh air.

Mrs Brewer and her daughter Janine took Sarah under their downy wings while Christie got things straight, and Janine was delighted when Christie offered to pay her to care for Sarah while she worked. Maudie Timms brought a box of groceries around. Canon Percival came round to murmur sweet nothings about Sunday School attendance and whist drives into Christie's ear. Ellen Brewer—née Jefferies—brought her little Tom around to play. Sooner or later the entire cast of villagers appeared, full of kind words and welcome. Everyone seemed to know exactly when Sarah's birthday was. But no one went so far as to ask who the father might be.

If Lucas Merrick was lighting anybody's fire, then he was doing it away from home. He was in Ireland, apparently, looking for a mare. When he came back, he came nowhere near the cottage. So it was all quite idyllic—apart from the fact that she still cried herself to sleep—until, early one morning, Sarah climbed the bars of a gate to look at the rider galloping by. And the rider looked at Sarah.

'Good morning.' Clipped. Short. Polished. The greeting of a handsome man in jodhpurs astride a fine horse.

'Hi, Lucas.'

'You gave me a start.'

'Really? I thought you must have found out by now that I'd moved back after all. It's been nearly a month.'

He shrugged. 'I'd heard. That wasn't what gave me the start.' He nodded at Sarah. 'You used to stand on that gate, waving. She looks exactly as you did.'

Sarah beamed up. 'Can I pat his nose?'

Lucas jumped out of the saddle and led the big horse close. Keeping a firm hold on the bridle, he reached across and took Sarah's fat little hand in his own big one and guided it to the bony planes of the horse's face. His auburn eyes glinted. His chin tilted as if to let the sun catch his words. 'You like horses, do you, young lady?'

'No. I don't *like* them. I *love* them.' And the child laughed at her version of a primitive joke.

Surprisingly, Lucas laughed too. 'It's the way you tell them,' he explained drily to the child, and Sarah beamed even more broadly.

'Why did the zebra cross the road?' she asked, inspired by his approval.

But when challenged by Lucas she proved to have forgotten the answer. 'You'll have to buy an ice-lolly,' she instructed him firmly. 'They have jokes on the sticks. Ask the lady in the shop to give you the lolly with the zebra joke on it. She'll know. She can read.'

And Lucas promised that he would, while Sarah reached out and gave the horse another reassuring little stroke.

'You used to get on my nerves when you wanted to pat their noses all the time,' he said coolly.

'I guessed.'

'You used to stroke upwards instead of down. Against the way the hair grows.'

'So I've been rubbing you up the wrong way since I was tiny? Tell me something new, Lucas.'

'Why did you come back?'

Christie was silent for a moment, then she nodded at Sarah. 'She's brown, isn't she? If you'd seen her when she arrived you'd have known why. She was pale and thin and she had a cough.'

'Pale and thin but not shy?'

'No. Sarah only *looks* like me. It can be deceptive. She's never been shy.'

'You grew out of it, though...' said Lucas caustically as he remounted.

'Yes.'

'In style.' There was that contempt again.

'If you say so, Lucas.'

Lucas just raised his eyebrows, and then nudged the big bay mare with his heels.

'I like that man,' said Sarah, watching him disappear.

'Do you, darling?' murmured Christie, watching him too, and wondering how she could ever have dreamed that he might come one day to love her. He'd been treating her with that same cruel indifference for almost as long as she could remember. To everyone else she knew she was a young woman, mature beyond her years in many ways, with a good career and a delightful child. In Lucas Merrick's eyes she was a contemptible schoolgirl still.

Sarah took to sitting on the gate for hours, looking out for the man on the horse. Christie let her do it, dodging out of sight as soon as Lucas appeared.

If she didn't make her escape with sufficient dispatch, Lucas would give her just the minutest of nods. No more than a flicker of his eyes, really. He reserved the dignity of the spoken word for Sarah.

'How do you do this fine morning, my lady?' he would ask, and Sarah would giggle and reach out to stroke whichever of his horses he was exercising, while Christie concentrated on keeping a faint, polite smile hovering somewhere in the vicinity of her mouth. Being snubbed like that hurt. Sometimes she suspected that he only made such a fuss of her daughter in order to emphasise his reserve where Christie was concerned. Then she felt like snatching Sarah away and forbidding her to talk to the man on the horse. But a deep sense of honour kept her resolutely smiling, though she kept her eyes lowered. This was Sarah's father, after all. She had a right to get to know him, even if he stubbornly refused to acknowledge any relationship to the child. Later, when Sarah was old enough to ask all the questions for herself, she wouldn't thank her mother for having denied her that chance. Anyway, she had to admit that Lucas seemed genuinely interested in little Sarah, and skilfully tempered his wry wit in the child's presence so that he invariably delighted her.

One day when Sarah was with Mrs Brewer and Christie was sitting at her computer keyboard she heard footsteps in the lane outside. The house sat right at the end of the lane, so that there was no such thing as a passer-by. She went to the window of the spare bedroom where she worked and looked out. It was Lucas, and he had a tear-stained Sarah sitting on his shoulders.

Christie tumbled down the narrow staircase and out through the front door.

'Sarah!' she exclaimed, studiously avoiding Lucas's disapproving gaze as he swung the child down and set her on the ground. 'Whatever's the matter, darling?'

'Janine's got a fat leg,' hiccuped Sarah, running into Christie's outstretched arms and bursting into tears.

Christie ran her tongue over her lips before summoning up the nerve to look enquiringly at Lucas for an explanation. Lucas's expression was predictably severe.

'She took Sarah out for a walk and fell and sprained her ankle,' explained Lucas. 'Luckily I rode by and Sarah had the presence of mind to chase after me. They'd been there for some time, from what Janine said. They were right out near the Dixons' place—too far for Janine to let Sarah go for help.'

'Thank you for bringing her back,' said Christie sincerely.

Lucas shrugged coldly. 'It was lucky she'd already made friends with me. If I'd been a stranger she probably wouldn't have had the confidence to run after me as she did.'

Christie gave a weak smile. 'Yes. Yes, it's lucky...' she echoed.

Lucas gave her a long, frozen look before saying, 'It was lucky, too, that it happened when she was out with Janine. If she'd been with you I doubt you'd have let her summon help from me, would you?'

Christie bit her lip. 'What makes you say that?' she said stiffly.

'I've seen you run indoors when I come into view. You're avoiding me.'

'Don't you think it's for the best, Lucas? I would have thought you'd be only too glad not to have to speak to me.'

Lucas tilted his head, and his eyes shone with a biting sharpness. 'What I fail to understand, Christabel, is your allowing Sarah to make friends with me at all. Most good mothers don't allow their children to befriend people they themselves avoid.'

So he didn't think she was a good mother? He couldn't have put it more bluntly if he'd tried. Encountering Lucas was a bit like lying on a bed of nails and waiting to be trampled. How much longer could she endure the pain of it? A bit longer, she thought with resignation, struggling to think of a conciliatory response. For Sarah's sake.

'I—er... To be honest, I thought of it in terms of her making friends with your animals—not with you. She loves horses. I used to be the same. I would have hated it if I'd been forbidden to pat their noses.'

'But your aunt liked *me*—she probably wouldn't have encouraged you to pester someone she disliked. And anyway, there are plenty of other horses hereabouts she could get to know.'

'You're the only one who rides past the house.'

'You're not answering my question.'

Christie turned her heated face upwards from her stooped position, cuddling the now calmed child. 'I... Look, if you want me to stop Sarah from waiting for you on the gate I will.'

'Mummy! No! Don't be so mean! Lucas said he'd give me a ride on his pony!'

Lucas reached out a long-fingered brown hand and rumpled the child's hair. 'It's OK, Sarah. I like our little chats. I don't want your mother to stop you waiting for me—and I'll fix up that ride just as soon as Janine's leg is better.'

'Really?' The delighted child grinned and pulled away from her mother's arms. She hugged Lucas's long, jeans-clad legs and then went dancing off into the house.

Christie watched her go, then turned back to Lucas, frowning. 'That's very kind of you, but you needn't bother.'

'I've promised her. It's no trouble. Janine can bring her up one morning. She's not badly injured. She'll be back on her feet before long.'

It was stupid to feel hurt. Honestly, what was the matter with her? She'd had years to get used to the fact that Lucas didn't want her around, and yet she still felt wounded by his obvious distaste for her company. 'Thank you,' she muttered ungraciously.

'So why haven't you told her not to pester me, Christie?'

Christie winced. She had hoped that that particular line of questioning had bit the dust. She should have known better. 'I've told you. She likes horses.'

'And I've told you that there are plenty of other horses near by. Every time you go to the village you pass two or three. Why aren't they the horses you encourage her to pet? Why mine?'

'I don't encourage her. She simply cottoned on to the fact that you rode past that gate every morning at about the same time. She's an intelligent child.'

'And you're an intelligent woman. Or are you trying to tell me that you don't exercise any control over your child?'

'Lucas! That's a dreadful thing to say. Look, I just remember—well, you were always very patient with me when I was small. I don't object to Sarah getting to know you. You don't have to stop if you don't want to.'

'No,' he agreed disdainfully. 'I don't. But I choose to. She's a great kid—she makes me laugh... And it must be good for her to have the opportunity to get to know a male of the species, especially since you've been cut off from your supply of city studs.'

Christie coloured deeply at the remark, and looked away so that he wouldn't see the pain which she was sure must be etched on to her features.

'Though as I remember,' drawled Lucas disparagingly, 'you didn't used to introduce them. You were waiting to meet a man who satisfied you between the sheets first. Is that why you're letting her get to know me? Is it an invitation, Christie?'

Christie gave a horrified exclamation. 'No! Of course not! Anyway, I told you before that it wasn't quite like that... I was... exaggerating.'

'Oh, yes. I recall your mentioning that now. And she does still see her father after all, doesn't she? Will he be coming down here to visit?'

'It's none of your business,' muttered Christie furiously. 'Now if you don't mind, Lucas, I have work to be getting on with. Thank you for bringing Sarah back and looking after her. I'm very grateful.'

But Lucas hadn't waited for her thanks. He had already turned on his heel and was walking away. Christie watched his receding figure with a bleak sense of despair. Why was he so determined to think that Sarah was James's child? You'd think he must have worked it out by now, a clever man like him. Too clever... that was the trouble. Too clever to allow himself to be lumbered with a responsibility he had never sought, and which he had gone to some pains to avoid. So why on earth was she still in love with a man like that?

Sarah plagued the life out of Christie over the promised ride. Janine's ankle was mending well, but it would be a couple of weeks before she was fully fit. Sarah flagged Lucas down one morning and grumpily told him that it had already been six days since he'd issued his invitation and the doctor had said it would be a hundred years before Janine was better, so couldn't Mummy bring her instead.

Christie closed her eyes and smiled a sickly smile. 'I didn't put her up to it,' she said between clenched teeth. 'And I'll explain it to her later. There's no problem.'

'Indeed there's not,' agreed Lucas sharply. 'Of course your mother can bring you. I'll see you this afternoon at two. I'll be in the stables at Home Farm.'

Christie could have screamed. Instead she fostered an illusion of excited anticipation for Sarah's sake, but had to acknowledge as two o'clock approached that she was relieved to find the weather was on her side. It had turned grey and blustery; a handful of yellow leaves danced in the air. With any luck it would rain and they could call the whole thing off.

But it didn't. And worse, when they arrived Lucas came out of the stable to greet them at the same moment that Soloman pricked his ears and whickered softly, and then cantered with what looked awfully like delighted recognition straight to Christie's side. He proceeded to nudge her affably with his nose. The pony's obvious affection brought tears to her eyes. She yearned to make a fuss of him, but Lucas was watching and she dared not get emotional with him around, so instead she stepped back and said briskly, 'What's happened to William?'

Lucas pulled a face. 'We lost him a couple of years back.'

Sarah glowered. 'Why don't you go and look for him, then?'

'Lucas means that he died, darling. He was very old.'

Sarah's scowl remained fixed in place. 'Huh. Then why didn't you bring me here *before* he died, Mum?' she asked accusingly, with all the self-centredness of extreme youth. 'You could have let me be born much sooner, and then I could have ridden William too. You're a mean, horrible person. I don't like you any more. I wish Lucas was my mummy instead.'

Christie winced, but Lucas let out a howl of laughter.

'What on earth has happened to your sense of humour, Christie?' he complained wryly. 'I can't believe that you're the girl who used to laugh so helplessly that she got the hiccups. Remember that time at the Amateur Dramatic Society production when Maudie played a consumptive and she had so much make-up on that——'

Christie put her hand over her mouth. 'Yes,' she mumbled, remembering not Maudie, but Lucas leading her stooped, fifteen-year-old form out of the church hall, and muttering something about a nasty tummy bug to the disapproving onlookers, while she shook and squawked, her hands pressed to her burning face. Outside they had lain on a roadside verge and had laughed together until their eyes had run with tears and their throats had ached. That was the last summer they had fooled around together like that. The following year Lucas had had a string of sophisticated girlfriends and no time at all to waste on a giggling schoolgirl.

'Is the tack still in the same place?' she asked stiffly. 'I can see to Sarah if you're busy.'

But the tack wasn't in the same place, because an impressive new stable block had been built, and Lucas, it appeared, wasn't to be allowed to be too busy, because Sarah wasn't having it. She took his hand and marched him off. Christie trailed in the background, her hands stuffed into her anorak pockets. She tried not to think about anything.

She almost cheered with relief when first one raindrop and then a second landed coldly on her head.

'Time to go,' she called brightly across at Sarah, who was plodding around in circles on Soloman's broad back, with Lucas holding the head collar.

He looked across at Christie. 'She's welcome to——'

But Christie interrupted crisply. 'It's going to rain. We'd better get a move on.'

Lucas looked at the sky, and held the palm of one hand out to test her assertion. Christie took the opportunity to lift Sarah off the pony's back.

'You're right,' conceded Lucas. 'Sorry about that, Sarah. We'll do it again some other time if you like.' He drew his car keys out of his pocket and offered them to her. 'The Range Rover's in front of the house,' he said brusquely. 'You go ahead while I get someone to see to Soloman.'

She neither wanted nor expected to be invited indoors, but Christie couldn't help but notice the snub implicit in his anxiety to get her off the premises.

'We can walk...' she protested coolly.

But Lucas simply shook his head. 'No need. I said I'd drop in on the Canon some time today for a game of chess. Now's as good a time as any. I can drop you off on the way.'

When the three of them were safely buckled in Christie commented, 'So you still play chess at the vicarage?'

'Yes. You used to enjoy going over there for a game yourself. You should invite yourself over. Percy'd like it.'

'You always got on so well with him...' Christie said, remembering.

'So did you. But then I defy anyone not to.'

'Yes. But you were... well, different when you were with him. At least,' she added hurriedly, hoping that he wouldn't have noticed the note of wistful nostalgia in her voice, 'when we used to play chess together over at the vicarage you were different. It was the game itself that affected your mood, I expect. You were absolutely brilliant.'

He gave a short laugh. 'You never did manage to beat me, Christie. Though you certainly played well enough. But then you turn out to be an expert player in quite a surprising number of fields, don't you?'

Christie bowed her head and let her fringe fall forward to shadow her eyes. She couldn't say anything in front of Sarah, but she knew exactly what he was talking about, and it *wasn't* chess. She sighed. She remembered playing chess with him as clearly as she remembered making love with him. He played cunningly, so that she had always been astonished when he forced her to resign just when she assumed she had him beaten at last. He was a born opportunist, she thought ruefully. Making comments like that in front of Sarah was just another example.

'Perhaps I will call on Percy for a game,' she said, changing tack. 'He's such a gentle soul.'

'Gentle?' Lucas sounded incredulous. 'That's only a façade, you know. Underneath he's as tough as they come. Percy tutored me for a year when I was expelled from my prep school. He was the only person who could manage me when I was a wilful twelve-year-old. In fact he gave me some very sound advice.'

Christie flinched. She remembered an occasion when they'd both been over at the vicarage and Percy had done just that. He'd been teasing Lucas about his string of girlfriends, referring to them as 'the house-martins—Lucas's summer visitors,' and then he'd rather gravely advised him that it was about time he settled down and got married. Lucas had flown into a rage and had been astonishingly rude to the mild-mannered clergyman, and then had stormed out, slamming the door so violently that a glass was shaken off the table in the sitting-room and shattered dramatically on the wood-block floor.

'I really can't imagine your *taking* his advice, though,' she challenged.

'Now that,' said Lucas surprisingly, 'is where you're wrong. I took his advice as a youngster and I find I still have a tendency to take his advice—*very* occasionally. Though I have to admit that I never do anything against my better judgement.' There was a pause and then he added acerbically, 'Though there have been one or two notable exceptions.'

Christie looked across at him. His was smiling bitterly. His eyes were fixed hard on the road ahead.

Suddenly she badly wanted to tell him that she was sorry. She would never have thrown herself at him that night if she hadn't honestly believed something so absurd that even thinking about it now made her hands fly to her face to cover her smile.

She sucked in her cheeks and bit on them. And yet it hadn't been funny at the time. She'd been so terribly innocent—that had been the trouble. She had known about the frogs and the birds and the bees. But she'd been brought up by a bookish man and an old countrywoman. They'd done a good job by and large. But there had never been a women's magazine lying on either of their sofas; never a racy novel on the bookcase, nor a tabloid newspaper discarded in front of the TV. In other words, until Christie had found herself in Lucas's arms, being kissed by him, her body moulded against his, her heart beating to the urgent pulse of his desire, sensing his need as his body quickened and hardened to the demanding rhythm of their kiss, she'd had no idea that what she had imagined might have happened was quite beyond the bounds of possibility. There was no way in the world she could have become pregnant from that other clumsy embrace, because James's lank frame had been every bit as unresponsive as her own.

But by the time she had found that out it was too late. Lucas was kissing her and her senses were on fire and she loved him so much that there was no way she could draw back...

CHAPTER FIVE

Lucas lifted Sarah out, but left Christie to jump down herself.

'Thanks for the lift,' she said politely. 'It was kind of you.'

Lucas stared at her. 'Kindness didn't come into it,' he returned brusquely.

'You offered against your better judgement, I suppose,' she snapped irritably.

He looked her up and down. 'I think I must have. Dear, dear... How careless of me. I'd better be watch out, hadn't I, Christie? We don't want to make any more...mistakes. Do we?'

'It takes two to make that kind of mistake, Lucas,' she said furiously. 'You may not trust your judgement, but I trust mine. You're quite safe.'

'Good.' He smiled, turning to get back into the car. '"Better safe than sorry" has never exactly been a governing precept in my life. But perhaps it's not such an offensive motto after all. In the right context.'

She had to exercise every ounce of her self-control to hide her anger from Sarah. The child liked Lucas. Christie had no right to start turning her against him—however unintentionally. And anyway, she was a fool to allow him to rile her so. She should be used to his manner by now.

He had been particularly cool towards her that summer. She'd no sooner arrived than she had run up to the stables adjoining the big, half-timbered manor-house, ostensibly to greet William and Soloman.

He had emerged from an outbuilding, rubbing his hands on the back of his jeans. 'Oh, lord,' he'd sighed, his face hardening the moment he caught sight of her. 'It's not that time of year again, is it? Time to start playing nursemaid.'

'Shut up, Lucas. That's an unfair thing to say. It's years since you've had to rescue me from one of my scrapes.'

'Is it? I'm sorry; it feels like just yesterday.'

'I...I'll clear off if you like. Only I thought you found it useful, having me to exercise the ponies.'

He looked her up and down, scornfully. 'You're a bit big for them these days.'

'I'm no taller than I was last year. Just a year older. I've left school now.'

'You've filled out. Puppy fat. You pubescent girls are all the same—you've a long way to go before you grow into a real woman, Christie. You're just an overweight kid, still.'

Christie tossed her head. Overweight kid! Huh! She had a good figure—everyone said so. She wasn't the least bit plump. 'If you think I'm too big to ride them, then say so. I'll stay away.'

He shrugged. 'You can ride them. But you won't find them up here at the stables. They've been moved to a paddock at Home Farm.'

'Reg and Lily Crabtree's farm?'

'My farm. The Crabtrees have retired. I've taken it on.'

'Who's living in the house?'

'Me. I'm renovating it.'

'Oh, how exciting! Can I come and look around?'

'Nope.'

'I'll go, then, shall I?'

'Yes. Let the grown-ups get on with their work.'

He avoided her like the plague. She took the opportunity of his ignoring her to go on a diet. Perhaps when he next bothered to turn his head in her direction she'd impress him with her model-girl slimness. She saw *him*, of course. Especially when she was down with the ponies. Lucas came back and forth to the farmhouse, often with a woman on his arm. He spent a great deal of time showing *them* his renovations.

One of them, an elegant creature with long golden hair, was a more frequent visitor than the others.

Christie was grooming William, bent low, hidden by the horse's bulk.

'Who's that girl who's always hanging around, Lucas?'

'The niece of one of the villagers. She's just a kid.'

'She looks past the age of consent to me.'

'Maybe. I don't keep track of her birthdays. She's just a kid with a crush on ponies. A bit of a pain, but I expect she'll grow out of it.'

'You sound as if you don't like her.'

'Quite honestly I've never considered the question. Why the interest, anyhow?'

'Just sizing up the competition, Lucas.'

'Competition? You must be joking... There's no competition when you're around, Lisa.'

'Ah... but what about when I'm not around?'

'Then come around more often. Stick around.'

'Is that a proposal?'

'Not the kind you mean, no.'

'Lucas, you're a rat. You want to have your cake and eat it.'

'Any reason why I shouldn't?'

'Some woman will catch you in the end, Lucas, tie you down with marriage and children. You're not immune.'

'Me? With a houseful of brats? Oh, no, Lisa. I don't like my women barefoot and pregnant. Not me.'

Christie sighed heavily when they had moved out of earshot. When was he going to notice that she had grown up? *When*?

The summer went from bad to worse. The skies were perpetually overcast that year, but she couldn't have cared less. Lucas didn't merely ignore her. If she appeared in his field of vision he pointedly turned his back. If she said hello, then he returned her greeting with a remark so cutting that it was as much as she could do to keep the tears from her eyes. And on top of that Aunt Sassy was told that she had rheumatoid arthritis and Maudie Timms shook her head very gravely and said, 'Oh, dear, that isn't good news at all, not at all,' and she told everyone in the shop that it wasn't good news, and Christie began to feel very alarmed.

She rang her father for consolation, but to her surprise Matron answered the phone. 'I've just popped over for a sherry with your father,' said Matron smugly. 'He gets very lonely at times.' Her father came to the phone. 'Rheumatoid arthritis?' he said vaguely. 'Oh, dear. That's not good news at all. We were hoping it would just be ordinary arthritis.' Christie had meant to ask him why it wasn't good news and why it was so much more dreadful than ordinary arthritis, but instead she found herself asking why Matron was in the house. 'Veronica?' he replied rather sheepishly. 'Oh, just a social visit. You know. She's a very cultured woman, is Veronica...'

'I hope she's drinking dry sherry,' muttered Christie. 'Tell her that sweet sherry isn't good for her teeth.' Matron made everyone's life a misery over the question of sugar, confiscating sweets and scrubbing the teeth of defaulters until their gums bled.

She rang her father again at eight-thirty the following morning. Matron answered the phone again. She asked, 'Did your father explain why I was here last night?'

'Yes...' lied Christie, not wanting to demean her father in the ghastly Veronica's eyes by revealing his cowardice... Anyway, he certainly didn't need to explain *now*. Anything that might have needed explaining about Matron's presence in the house at eight-thirty in the evening was so abundantly clear at eight-thirty in the morning that any attempt at explanation would be quite superfluous.

'I hope you don't mind.'

'Why should I?'

'A lot of girls your age would take a very different view, I fear—especially if they were motherless only children.'

'Could I speak to my father?'

'I'm afraid he isn't available to come to the phone. Can I take a message?'

No. No message. She tried once more at three that afternoon. When Matron answered yet again she set the receiver back in its cradle without speaking a word. As far as Christie could tell there was nothing at all left to look forward to in life. Aunt Sassy was apparently gravely ill, even though she only seemed to have a stiff knee, and her father was going to marry that ghastly Veronica, and they would never ever again have honey on their bread for tea. Not that she'd want to eat tea in her father's house if Matron was there pouring out. And worst of all she was starting her computer course in September and there'd be no more summers and no more Lucas, and she'd be quite, quite alone in the world and her heart would break.

The only thing left to look forward to was the party up at the manor. The major hosted an enormous, gloomy party in honour of his wife's birthday at the end of August every year. The villagers were invited with due condescension to come along and rub shoulders with the gentry, and, tongue in cheek, they turned up in droves and made sure they had an excellent time. But even that was weeks away, and in the meantime Christie had nothing at all to console her.

'Good lord. It's Superbrat!' jeered Lucas when she turned up to ride Soloman.

'Do you get all your kicks from being offensive?'

'I'm afraid that rather depends on the company I'm forced to keep. Given more mature companionship, I'm capable of deriving a considerably more mature level of gratification. It's only you that brings out the juvenile delinquent in me, Christie. I wonder why that can be.'

She felt wretched from the moment she woke up to the moment she fell asleep. The diet had been forgotten, but it didn't matter, because she'd lost her appetite anyway. Even the sight of food made her feel sick. Food meant home and warmth and comfort and love, and as far as she could see her future held precious little of any of them—especially love. The daily encounters with Lucas were getting increasingly unbearable.

On the morning of the party itself she took a currycomb to William's coat with unusual vigour. Lucas was in his house, and Lisa's car was parked in the driveway. It was six a.m. Obviously, like Matron, she was a woman who liked to get her social calls over with early in the day.

'Woah... Steady on...' Lucas's voice cut across the crisp morning air.

She turned towards the direction of the sound. He was sauntering across the dew-dusted grass, a harsh frown on his face. He lifted one hand to brush his dark hair back from his brow. 'You should know better,' he snapped. 'You've groomed them often enough.'

'I'm sorry,' she said stiffly. 'I'll go a little more gently.'

'I'm fond of these old ponies,' he continued ruthlessly. 'I don't like to think of them being mistreated.'

'Lucas, I've said I'm sorry! I was being a little rough, I'll admit, but I wasn't mistreating them.'

'No? I suppose not. But don't let it happen again or I shall have to ask you not to come any longer.'

'You don't need to worry,' she returned bitterly. 'I'm leaving the day after tomorrow. And I shan't be back next summer. I've grown up, Lucas. I shall have started work by then. You've nothing to fear. This is the last summer you'll be seeing me.'

He looked at her with a cold anger in his eyes. 'Good!' he bit out, and then turned on his heel and went back to the house, where Lisa, no doubt, would be busy spreading honey on his toast so thickly that it trickled off the sides...

Christie sighed heavily when he moved out of earshot. He would never notice that she had grown up now. There wasn't even any point in her putting on that lovely black dress with the shoe-string straps and the tiny buttons and going to the party. There was no hope left at all.

She turned and made her way mournfully back to the cottage, mooning up in her bedroom, peering at her reflection in the old, ugly mirror. What was the matter with her? She should have everything in life to look forward to. She was an attractive young woman... Though now she came to think of it the monthly evidence of her womanhood had been strangely absent this summer. Not that it need concern her. It wasn't as if she had anything to worry about. She'd only ever been kissed once in her entire life, and, goodness only knew, that had been an innocent enough business. The days when girls believed you could get pregnant just from a kiss were long gone! She couldn't possibly have got *pregnant* from that embarrassing encounter with James Lakey. The idea was laughable. One silly kiss—that was all it had been. Though they *had* ended up sort of half lying down, and her dress had got rucked up and James had got himself very hot and bothered...

But it had just been a kiss. Hadn't it? Of course it had! Honestly, these past six weeks were beginning to addle her brain. It had just been a *kiss*. Of course. Though it *had* been dark, and she had been too squashed and uncomfortable to pay much attention to anything other than her precarious breathing, but, even so, *nothing* had happened.

And then she remembered something else. Sex education hadn't exactly featured high on the list of priorities in the small girls' school she had attended. It had been left till the sixth form. But by then she'd been at Braizeneath. There *had* been a lesson of sorts. The gruff, grey-haired biology master had done a lot of drawings of frogs on the blackboard. The boys had all laughed. The girls had tried to appear super-cool, rolling their eyes and pursing their lips. Of course, they all knew quite a lot about it anyway. You couldn't grow up in this modern world without knowing the facts of life. But the teacher—used to addressing boys—had said something which had stuck in her mind.

'Remember the tadpoles, lads. Remember what good little swimmers they are. Well, in comparison, the male reproductive cell is an Olympic champion. You take care when you start paying court to young ladies, my boys. Truth can be stranger than fiction. Just remember that those little tadpoles of yours can complete the last leg of the journey all by themselves.'

It couldn't be true, could it? It was just the sort of thing an old buffer like him *would* say to put the fear of God into the boys. No. It couldn't possibly be true. Especially as nothing had happened... But still her mouth parched with fear every time she remembered. What if one of those tadpoles had escaped, after all, and turned out to be a better swimmer than even the biology master could have imagined?

Christie did nothing all day, to Aunt Sassy's annoyance. When she went down for lunch it was her favourite cheese soufflé, but she couldn't manage more than a few mouthfuls.

'What's the matter with you?' her aunt scolded.

'Nothing,' she replied leadenly, trying to force down another mouthful. *I hope*, she added mentally, her heart jumping with fear. Nothing. There was nothing the matter. But if there was nothing the matter, then why couldn't she eat? Why had her periods stopped? Oh, it was the craziest thought she'd ever had in all her life. She was just an ordinary person. For something like that to happen you'd need to be one in a billion. And she wasn't one in a billion. She was just ordinary. Except that it wasn't so very ordinary to have your father fall in love with the nastiest woman in the world quite unexpectedly over a glass of sherry. Or for your darling aunt to get stricken down with a peculiar sort of sore knee which meant that she probably didn't have long to live. Or to have lost your mother at birth... Or to be so totally in love with a man much older than you—a man who actually hated the very sight of you—that you thought your heart was going to break...

None of those things were the least bit ordinary. And now she had to get ready for this wretched party knowing that she was the only eighteen-year-old virgin who'd only ever been kissed once in all her stupid life and got pregnant as a result. Good grief. She'd have to bring up the child single-handedly, and Lucas would hear about it and despise her worse than ever, and she'd never, ever, *ever* know what it was like to love Lucas and be loved in return.

She cried her heart out in the bath, and then shut her bedroom door resolutely behind her. Right. Where was that dress? And the make-up she'd bought. And the high-heeled shoes with the little bows on the front. Fate might have played a dirty trick on her, but tonight she was going to fight back. Just once, she told herself as she waved the mascara wand inexpertly between her face and the mirror. Please let him make love with me just this once and I shall resign myself to my fate for the rest of my days.

The party was in full swing by the time she arrived, and it took her quite a while to locate Lucas. He was leaning nonchalantly against a wall, looking stunning in a white dinner-jacket. She looked up at him and smiled uncertainly. 'Hi, Lucas,' she said.

He tilted his head to one side, pushed his floppy hair back from his face, and gave her a vague half-smile in return. 'Have you got a drink? Let me get someone to see to you—your friends from the village are all living it up in the great hall, I think.'

The relentless thump of the disco could be heard everywhere. She had already glimpsed Ellen and Tommy dancing with each other in the big, oak-panelled room. She had ignored them intentionally, determined to find Lucas before her courage failed.

'It's OK,' she said hurriedly, then blazed out a frightened smile. 'It was you I wanted to see, Lucas...'

She wished she hadn't said that. It was so stupid and obvious—she ought to have said something subtle, and just a little flirtatious. But she didn't know how to talk that way. Her mind went blank as she searched for something appropriate...

'Oh?' he drawled. His eyes were glancing over her head as if he was desperate to find someone else to talk to.

'Yes,' she continued blindly. 'I wanted to speak to you. Er—you see...'

His hand came up to touch her elbow in a formal little gesture of dismissal. 'Christie, if you don't mind, I——'

'It's about Soloman... It's really important...' she gabbled, almost in a panic. Oh, she was crazy. He wasn't the least bit interested in her and yet here she was attempting to play out this stupid fantasy of seducing him. Her eyes stung with a sharp pain, and when she blinked she expected to find them moist, but fear had kept them scratchily dry.

'Yes...?' he enquired vaguely, still not meeting her eye.

'Well, I looked in on him earlier and he seemed to be in bad shape...' Her heart lurched as she recognised the enormity of the lie which had just left her lips. For a moment her mouth dried completely and her tongue seemed stuck to her palate. She swallowed hard. 'He was sweating, and making dreadful noises, and I sort of thought... You know... Isn't that a symptom of...of—er—something serious, Lucas?'

Lucas frowned, and then gave her his full attention. 'Was he standing up?' he asked.

Christie shook her head, and then changed her mind and began nodding. 'No. Well, that is, yes. But he was sort of staggering a bit as if he might lie down. You know the sort of thing.'

He caught hold of her upper arm. For a moment his fingers bit hard against her flesh and then he let go. 'When was this? How long ago?'

Christie took a deep breath. Oh, dear. When would Lucas have last seen him? She had to make it sound later than that...'

'Er—I don't know exactly. Not long ago...'

'On your way over here?'

'Yes...' Now that was ridiculous. How could she have possibly seen the animal in a pair of glintingly new high-heeled shoes? 'Well, a bit before, actually. I went for a long walk and then realised I was late and dashed home and changed.'

'You silly girl,' he muttered as he dragged her along behind him. 'You should have come to tell me right away...'

They went to Home Farm on his motorbike, roaring through the summer dusk. She had to hold him tightly around the waist. She pressed her cheek against his back and felt the breadth of muscle and bone beneath his immaculate dinner-jacket. She was frightened and excited at the same time.

When they pulled up at the paling alongside the paddock Lucas leapt anxiously off the powerful machine, and narrowed his eyes to survey the pony in the gathering dusk.

'There's nothing whatsoever wrong with that animal,' he said.

Christie had come to stand beside him. 'Er—he certainly looks better now... from a distance,' she agreed weakly.

Lucas stooped a little to look keenly into her eyes. His face tightened into furious lines. He didn't say a word; he just went on looking into her eyes.

'Um...' she said. 'Um...'

And then Lucas straightened up and threw back his head and let out a great gust of laughter. 'Why did you say it?' he said at last.

'I—er...'

And then he put his hands on her shoulders and looked down on her blushing cheeks and said, 'What wonderfully honest eyes you have, Christie.'

'Have I?' she whispered.

'Why did you bring me here?'

'I—er—I wanted to see you on your own,' she admitted shakily.

'What for?'

It was now or never. Quaking with fear, she stood on tiptoe and lifted one arm to the back of his neck. Then she turned her face to his and pulled his head down. 'For this...' she breathed as his mouth met hers.

She didn't know what she had expected. Certainly she hadn't expected such an instantaneous, fiery response. His mouth tutored hers with a speed she wouldn't have imagined possible. He kissed her deeply and passionately; and excitedly, intuitively, she began to kiss him back. Within moments arousal began to surge like a great tide inside her. She moved closer to him, feeling the hard planes of his body beneath her hands.

Abruptly he pulled his head away. 'For crying out loud...' he groaned, pushing her away. 'Is that what you wanted, Christie?'

She stared frantically into his angry eyes. Already her awakened body was quivering with need. 'I...' She took a deep, ragged breath. 'No. Kiss me again, Lucas...' she pleaded.

He caught hold of her then and dragged her close. His mouth covered hers with uncommon speed. His barbed chin raked across her skin as he bruised her mouth with an even more demanding kiss. She closed her eyes and melted into his arms. After what seemed like a very long time he drew his head back, but continued to hold her close.

'That's enough...' he said.

She shook her head. She had forgotten what had brought her here. Oh, yes... that silly notion that she was one in a billion... Her vow... All that was lost as the darkness gathered about her. She was in his arms and he had kissed her and she wanted him to go on kissing her and she couldn't bear to end what had only just begun. 'Please, Lucas...' she whispered. 'Don't stop.'

He half carried her into the house. It smelled of new paint and raw wood. One of the downstairs rooms was sparsely furnished. There was a bed. She couldn't remember how they got on to the bed, or anything further of her surroundings. She only remembered Lucas: Lucas kissing her so tenderly; Lucas discarding his jacket and his bowtie; Lucas with his auburn eyes, half hooded, his thick hair falling over his brow; Lucas unfastening the tiny buttons on her dress with shaking fingers; Lucas resting his head briefly on her breast.

'You are beautiful...' he murmured. 'The most beautiful creature I have ever set eyes upon.' And she looked at him and yearned to say the same, but she was too shy.

Later he lay beside her in the rumpled bed and said, 'Why did you ask me to kiss you?'

Christie ran her tongue nervously over her lips. How on earth could she answer him? It had seemed so plain before his mouth had met hers. And then, when she had realised what a fool she had been, it was far, far too late. She loved Lucas and she needed him, and oh, it had been so glorious and she just hadn't been able to draw back.

'I...' Her voice was croaky. She cleared her throat and started again, trying to think herself back into the mental state she had occupied less than an hour before. But all those wretched doubts had fled. When she had come to the party, determined to make Lucas notice her, she had been in the depths of despair. She had honestly believed the unbelievable. She had thought that her life was about to come crashing down around her. Now she was sublimely happy. She loved Lucas and they had made love and her body had trembled and shaken with the ecstasy of becoming one with him.

'I...just did...' she said lamely.

'There must have been a reason,' he persisted, frowning.

She swallowed. What if he guessed that she loved him? It would be dreadful... He hadn't asked for any of this, after all. He didn't even like her. 'A reason?' she echoed haltingly. 'Oh, yes. Well, it just seemed like a good idea at the time. You know...'

'Christie, what if you get pregnant?'

She sat up abruptly, then lay back down equally abruptly. 'I can't get pregnant,' she muttered. It would be too unfair on Lucas. That was why. Oh, lord, what on earth had she done?

'Look, Christie——'

'I shan't get pregnant, Lucas. It's out of the question. You can put the notion right out of your mind.'

He was silent for a long time. Then he said, 'You'd tell me if you were, wouldn't you?'

'There won't be anything to tell,' she said determinedly, pressing her lips hard together. She was the biggest idiot on the face of the earth, but she'd promised herself that she'd live uncomplainingly with the consequences of this night, and so she would. And as long as she had this precious time in Lucas's arms to remember, she would never, ever have a single regret.

CHAPTER SIX

CHRISTIE had gone back to her father's the following day, and accepted his meek apologies for letting Matron use her stereo system to re-record her huge collection of records on to tape. She could quite see how it would have been awkward for him to refuse, and why he had had to skulk outside for hours rather than share the house with her. Especially as she complained at his taking sugar in his tea.

Then she went to London to stay with Great-Aunt Irene and her unmarried daughter Letty. After a while she went to see a very nice doctor called Dr Hughes, who explained that it was quite common to miss periods on holidays or in times of emotional turmoil. He also explained that she was very slightly pregnant. A matter of weeks. She longed to tell Lucas, but stuck by her vow to face her future with good heart, though she hadn't anticipated how hard it would be, nor how much her heart would ache as it learned to be good.

It was Letty who insisted that she come down to Gloucestershire one fine Sunday to visit Aunt Sassy. She was a brusque woman—a dedicated nursing sister in her forties—and she brushed Christie's objections aside as if they were the whinings of an irritable toddler. Lucas found her sitting disconsolately in the woods behind the house.

'Christie...' His voice was almost tender—as if he understood her hurt and pitied her for it, as you might pity an animal in pain. He had always been kind to animals.

'Oh. Lucas. Hello...' She felt her face colour, and blinked furiously to dispel the image which clouded her vision. The last time she had seen him he had been naked, beside her in his bed.

'Thank goodness I've found you. I was going to come up to London to see you, but I heard you'd be here today.'

'Really?' Oh, silly, silly heart. It was jumping up and down with excitement. He had come to find her! The one strangulated word was all she could manage.

He came and sat next to her on the trunk of a felled tree. Her legs dangled childishly, one on each side of the fat trunk. Lucas's long legs stretched out in front of him, his feet firmly on the ground. Christie hung her head and looked at them and burned with love for him.

'Christie...?'

'Yes...?'

'You know you said you couldn't possibly have become pregnant? Well, I wanted to make sure...'

Oh. So that was why he had come looking for her. He wanted to make certain he was off the hook. She took a deep breath before replying, but the breath shuddered and shook her anguished frame, and the words got lost on their way out.

'You *are* pregnant, aren't you?' he asked, his voice suddenly sharp.

She nodded.

'Then I shall take full responsibility——'

'No!' she shouted out the word. 'No, Lucas. It's *not* your responsibility!' She had chased him shamelessly. She had promised herself that she would give up all her foolish dreams. It wasn't Lucas's fault. He mustn't be made to bear the burden of what had happened. 'It's not your fault.'

'Not my fault?'

She took a deep breath. 'Er—it's not your baby, you see...'

He looked at her, his eyes narrowed, as if every ounce of his intelligence was concentrated in their dark pupils. 'What? That can't be true...' he said incredulously.

'It is, Lucas.' She sighed and then looked into his face. She'd got herself into this stupid mess. It was nothing to do with him—his lovemaking had been a salve, a sweet, soothing ointment on a self-inflicted wound. She couldn't let him take the blame. She would tell him what she had believed to be the truth when she had asked him to kiss her. She would tell him that she was having Lakey's baby.

'Honestly, Lucas. There's this boy—James Lakey— at Braizeneath... Honestly, he's really nice—very kind and everything—and I'm very fond of him and, well, you see...' She took another gulping breath. 'I'm having *his* baby.'

Lucas's face had creased into appalled lines. 'A boy? A schoolboy? And is he going to marry you, Christie? For God's sake...'

'He's got a place at Oxford this term, so we won't be getting married,' she said stiffly. 'He's very clever and he's got a scholarship... He's an only child, and his parents think the world of him, so——'

'So he's going to walk away scot-free!'

'No! Lucas, really this isn't any of your business, but it isn't a bit like *that*. You see, Lakey—er—James...he couldn't be nicer, actually, and if he knew I'm sure he'd want to do the right thing... But, you see, it's *my* decision—I don't want him tied down and his life ruined——'

'So you'll ruin your own life instead? Like some sacrificial lamb?'

'No! My life *won't* be ruined! Don't you see? It's not going to be like that!'

This would be Lucas's baby. She felt astonishingly privileged to be having his child. And anyway, her father and her aunt hadn't had their lives ruined by having to bring up a child single-handed, had they? Christie bitterly resented the idea that *her* life would be ruined by having a baby to love and cherish—far from it. It had been a shock, certainly—but that didn't mean she wouldn't love her baby and make a happy life for them both.

'Then what *is* it going to be like, Christie?' said Lucas angrily. 'Just tell me that.'

'It's all going to be fine, believe it or not—because that's how I *choose* it to be,' she bit out furiously. 'It's my body—my baby—and I have the right to do exactly as I want!'

'Oh, no, you don't!'

'I do, Lucas. I think a very great deal of... of James, and I shall do what I think is right for both of us. I've made up my mind.'

There was a long silence. The air in the wood smelt moist and loamy. The sunshine above the canopy of the trees showered down between the leaves and branches in shattered fragments. All the birds stopped singing.

At last Lucas said, 'Take my advice, Christie. Have the baby adopted.'

'Adoption?' She looked at him in pained disbelief. He wanted her to have his baby adopted? What if her father had taken that decision? Good grief, it didn't bear thinking about! 'You can't be serious. Put myself through nine months of pregnancy only to spend the rest of my life worrying about the future of my baby? Oh, no, Lucas. Now that really would ruin my life!'

He gave her a glacial look. The blood seemed to creep in her veins. Her nerves prickled. She loved him so very much, but they were worlds and worlds apart. The only kind of woman he would ever be interested in was mature, glamorous and childless. She must have been a fool ever to have dreamt otherwise. But she was growing up very fast now. Soon she would put away her dreams for good... for her baby's sake as much as her own.

He gave a contemptuous shrug. 'It won't matter who raises it, Christie, as long as it has plenty of love. An adoptive family will provide love in abundance. You can put it behind you then...'

Christie turned her head to one side and looked upwards. She found herself staring hard at a young tree from which a branch had recently been ripped. The wound was pale against the grey bore of the trunk, the broken shards of wood sappy and green. 'No chance, Lucas. I'll do this my way.'

There was a long silence, and then twigs crackled as Lucas got to his feet. She turned and looked at him. He met her eyes with a disdainful reluctance, then his thumbs locked themselves into the belt of his jeans in a gesture of insolent dismissal. 'Be seeing you, Christie...' he said slowly, and she could tell from his voice that he hoped he wouldn't.

'Yeah,' she returned softly, her mouth dry, her eyes aching from the need to cry.

Autumn was beautiful in the countryside. Sarah started at the little village playgroup, and the morning walks through the drifts of golden leaves, the sharp air mellowing as the big sun rose higher, became Christie's solace for having moved back to Lucas's part of the world.

Sarah missed out on Lucas's morning chats, though, until one day, as they sauntered out into the lane outside the house, they found him sitting patiently on a big, dappled filly, just the other side of the five-bar gate.

'Hi, Sarah.' He smiled, and doffed his hard hat.

'Lucas!' Sarah ran up to the gate and clambered on the bars. 'Why are you here?'

He kept his eyes fixed on the child, while Christie edged nervously nearer.

'Because I missed your company. I decided to rearrange my schedule so that I come past this spot a little earlier each morning.'

'You mean I can see you every day?'

Christie gulped. It meant that she would have to see Lucas every day, too. She could hardly dodge back into the house when she was supposed to be walking Sarah to playgroup.

'Unless your mother disapproves.'

Christie bit her upper lip. 'Why should you take my feelings into account?' she asked archly.

He looked coolly at her. 'I don't believe in subverting a parent's authority over a child.'

'No. Right... Well, that's very kind of you, Lucas.' And then with a flash of spirit she continued, 'You've really changed, Lucas! Good grief—*you* used to be no respecter of parental authority. How staid you are becoming.'

Lucas's face hardened briefly, and then it suddenly and heart-rendingly broke into one of its fleeting smiles, his chin tilted upwards to catch the sun. 'No, I didn't, did I? Perhaps I am growing like my father after all. He always used to tell me I'd end up like him in the end. "You'll see, m'boy! When you're my age, you'll know exactly what I mean, and you'll be sorry for all you've put the old man through..."'

He was such a good mimic that she couldn't help laughing. 'You may have changed, Lucas,' she exclaimed, 'but you'll never change *that* much. The idea of you ending up like your father is...' She tailed off, realising that she had been about to be dreadfully rude about Lucas's father. They had used to mock him, a long, long time ago. 'Er—anyway, how are your parents? I haven't seen them since I moved back.'

Lucas frowned as swiftly as he had smiled. 'Very well, Miss Barnes, thank you kindly,' he said tauntingly. 'The major has a touch of gout now and then, and my mother suffers from it more than she deserves, but otherwise they are in excellent health.'

'I'm—er—pleased to hear it... Do give them my regards...'

And then Lucas's expression changed again, so that he looked unaccountably angry with her. 'I don't know who the hell *you're* going to end up like, Christie,' he muttered disparagingly. 'The speaking clock, maybe? All empty, courteous formality? You always used to ask after my parents in the old days, but then you used to say, "And how are the miserable old pair today?"'

Christie sucked on her lower lip. She didn't know whether she wanted to laugh or cry. 'I'm more mature these days, Lucas.'

'So I understand...'

'Oh, stop saying things to me in that tone of voice! Is it so unnatural that I should want to set my daughter an example of politeness?'

'Sarah isn't the least bit polite.'

'Lucas!'

'Now don't explode! She has delightful manners—it's just that they are, as yet, still uncorrupted by the demands of the world. She is, I'm delighted to say, as forthright as any other child her age, and I find it very amusing too. But she's certainly not polite, and I'm sure she wouldn't notice anything that you said to me—so long as it didn't concern *her*.'

'Are you looking for an excuse for being rude to me in her presence?'

Lucas shook his head. 'I never look for excuses for anything I do, Christie. Anyway, whatever I say to you goes straight over her head.'

There was certainly some truth in that. Sarah's ears seemed to be tuned to her own name, and certain other trigger words like 'ice-cream'—but there was still a lot that she was too young to take in. Even so, Christie resented his assertion that he never sought excuses for his own actions. After all, he was letting himself off the hook when it came to acknowledging his possible paternity of Sarah, wasn't he? No doubt he told himself that as he'd made all the proper noises at the time it was therefore no longer any concern of his. And what was *that* if it wasn't an excuse?

'Come on, Sarah,' she said, her voice suffused with annoyance. 'We shall be late.'

He rode away while Sarah waved. Christie wondered whether he would, indeed, be there to greet them the next morning. He hadn't looked as if he wanted to be.

The question proved academic. It started raining that afternoon, continued pouring down in the night, and was still raining torrentially the next morning. Christie bundled a protesting Sarah into the car and ran her to school. When she went to collect her the rain was still lashing down, the sky thick and grey, and the road slippery with sodden leaves. It rained all weekend. On Sunday, when she went to fetch in fresh logs for the fire they were drenched and wouldn't catch. She felt guilty about not having yet ordered any coal—but the weather had been so mild that it hadn't seemed important. She found a dusty electric fire and plugged it in.

It was still pouring down when night fell. Christie made a few anxious excursions to inspect the bedroom ceilings, but the roof didn't seem to have sprung any leaks. She got Sarah ready for bed, though the little girl was reluctant to go upstairs.

'I can hear too much pitter-pat,' she complained. 'It's too loud.'

It was something of a relief when someone knocked on the door. Ellen, probably. She'd promised to drop by with a book.

It was Lucas. His hair was plastered to his brow, and rain dripped off the end of his nose. His green waxed jacket gleamed, and puddles sat in the creases of the sleeves.

'Can I come in, or are you going to stand there staring at me all night?'

'Oh. Sorry. Yes, come in...'

Lucas took a few long strides into the room, then stopped to unbutton his jacket and ease his heavy-duty wellingtons off his feet.

'I saw the lights. I was surprised. I thought you might have gone to Percy's.'

'The vicarage? Why? We're quite safe and sound here.'

But Lucas didn't bother to answer. He had removed his gear, dropping it on to the doormat, where it could do least damage, and had crouched down to greet Sarah, who came running towards him. 'Hi, Lucas! Did you come to see my hot-water bottle? Remember I told you about it?'

'Of course. I remember everything you tell me. I thought you'd be bound to use it on a night like this.'

'Mummy said it was for winter when she bought it, but it's only autumn, isn't it? I know because we did it at playgroup with leaves.'

'Uh huh...' He stood up and took the little girl by the hand, leading her into the room. Then he turned to Christie and gave her one of his acerbic frowns. 'What's happened to the fire? It's cold in here.'

Christie pulled a guilty face. 'The wood's all soaked, and I haven't got round to ordering coal yet. I'll get some from the petrol station tomorrow.'

'No, you won't. The lane is impassable. That's why I was surprised you were still here.'

'The lane? But that's incredible... What's happened? Has a tree come down?'

Lucas shook his head impatiently. 'The river's burst its banks. Honestly, Christie, don't you ever switch on the radio?'

'Yes, but... Well, I was listening to a concert on Radio Three. They didn't say anything...'

'Local radio. Everybody in the countryside listens to it in unusual weather conditions. They've been warning that this might happen all day.'

Christie looked frantically around the room. 'Should we move everything upstairs? It's lucky there aren't any fitted carpets, and the floors are quarry-tiled, but... oh, what a shame, I gave this room a coat of emulsion just last week——'

'Hold it...' Lucas's arm shot out and his hand came to rest on her shoulder. 'The house won't get flooded.

It's too high. But the roads are. You're completely cut off.'

She should have been relieved that the house wasn't in any danger, but the presence of his fingers was unnerving her badly. She sensed the warmth of his skin, and realised that she had become as chilled as the room and was as daunted by the incessant pitter-pat as her daughter. She wanted to turn to him and lean against him. Instead she flinched, shrugging herself free of his hold.

'Oh. Good. But if the roads are blocked, then how did you get here?'

'On my motorbike. I took it out to the top fields to bring in some of the colts who needed shelter. I saw your lights on and came down. I had to wade across the lane, though.'

'Oh.' Christie frowned. 'Thank you. That was kind, but we're all right.'

'No, you're not. You haven't any dry wood, and the place is cold. How are you for food? You might be stranded for a few days.'

'Fine,' she said decisively.

But he paid no attention to her and marched out to the kitchen. He opened the fridge, and then stuck his head into the pantry. 'Half a loaf of bread, a quarter of a pint of milk and no more than half a dozen tins. Really, Christie, you aren't very well provisioned, you know.'

'I don't need to be,' she complained bitterly. 'Maudie's shop isn't far. That will do us until the milkman...' She tailed off. 'We won't die if we go twenty-four hours without milk.'

Lucas just gave her a withering look. 'I'll be back,' he said, making his way swiftly to the door.

Sarah ran after him. 'Look! I got him out of my bed to show you. He's not really a kangaroo. If you open his head you'll see the bottle.'

Lucas stopped and bent to examine the fluffy prize. 'He,' said Lucas firmly, taking the baby kangaroo out of the pouch, 'is a she. That's the nicest hot-water bottle cover I've ever seen.'

Sarah beamed with pride. 'It's better than central heating. And cheaper. Mummy said so.'

Lucas nodded seriously at the little girl, and then threw a sharp glance at Christie over the child's head. 'Mummy knows everything there is to know about keeping warm in bed. She's an expert,' he murmured sarcastically.

Christie felt her cheeks flaming. She pressed her tongue hard behind her teeth. She could hardly respond to his gibe without sparking off an exchange which would certainly set the child's ears wagging, and he knew it! The man was the worst kind of opportunist.

'Off to bed now,' ordered Lucas as he tugged on his wellingtons, and he smiled firmly at the child.

Christie couldn't help noticing a warmth in the man's eyes. He genuinely liked Sarah—despite his general dislike of children. But then, thought Christie, looking adoringly at her daughter's tiny figure, obediently mounting the stairs, Sarah was a peculiarly attractive child. Oh, she knew all mothers thought their own children were especially lovable, but she really did think that Sarah was an exception. Lucas might hate children in general, but she'd defy anyone to dislike her own precious lamb. Actually, he had always been tolerant of her, too, in a scornful, superior kind of way when she was just a small child. It was when she had become older and more gangly that he had started to show his loathing more openly.

She tried to settle down with the television, but it was hopeless. Her ears were straining for the sound of Lucas's bike beyond the relentless drumming of the rain. She remembered the stir he had first caused when he had walked out of his famous public school before his final exams, and had bought himself his first motorbike. He used it exclusively for riding around the huge acreage of farmland attached to the family estate, which he had taken to managing with uncommon flair. He'd soon provided himself with a zippy little sports car for the open road on the proceeds of his endeavours. The villagers had been thin-lipped. Aunt Sassy had laughed. Christie had been too young to understand what all the fuss was about. If she were Lucas she'd have bought a pony and trap.

She was getting badly worried when at last she heard a knock at the door. It was him, wetter than before, and with a large holdall slung over his shoulder.

'I didn't hear the bike...' she said, surprised, as he barged into the room, dropping the bag with a heavy thud.

'Water's got into the engine. It got me back to Home Farm, but wouldn't start when I was ready for the return journey,' he said coolly. 'I brought this lot on foot.'

She looked at him in surprise. 'Good grief. But you could have rung. We're not exactly destitute. I told you we could manage.'

He just gave her a frozen look, and held out his jacket to her. 'Put that somewhere to dry,' he said.

'I can't. There's only the electric fire.'

'Put it over the hot-water tank.'

'It's off until the morning. I used the last of the hot water for Sarah's bath. The water heater's on a time switch.'

He sighed, took his jacket back from her, and threw it in a heap on the quarry-tiled kitchen floor. He padded across the room in his socks, taking the holdall with him, and knelt in front of the hearth.

'I'll get a good fire going. If you bring in plenty of logs you can stack them at the side of the fireplace. They should be dry enough to light tomorrow.'

'But won't the roads be open tomorrow? It can't go on raining for much longer, surely?'

He didn't bother to reply immediately. His strong, dextrous hands were swiftly extracting dry kindling and fire-lighters from the bag, and arranging them deftly in the grate. To her surprise she found that he had a hundredweight bag of coal in there as well. He eased it out and sat it next to the scuttle.

At last he leaned back on his heels as the fire caught hold and said, 'The forecast is for more of the same. Even when the rain stops it could take a couple days for the lane to clear. It's happened before.'

'Yes. I sort of remember now. But I can never remember it having been a problem.'

'Most people who are at risk of being cut off have the sense to keep the house well stocked.'

Christie sighed. She remembered the hoard of tinned food and milk she had found when she had come down in May. She had eaten it all. There was enough food for a day or so, but little else. 'I don't need your help, Lucas,' she said sulkily. 'I could have walked over the fields to the shop if I was stuck.'

'It's nearly four miles over the hill—which is the only way not flooded—and four miles back. And the ground is very wet underfoot. Given that you'd probably have to give Sarah a piggy-back, just exactly how many pints of milk were you planning to carry? Anyway, you'd still have to wade across the lane. I wouldn't fancy doing that with a bag of shopping and a tired, cold child. You have no idea what it's like out there.'

Christie sighed again. Lucas had a way of implying that she really wasn't up to the task of caring properly for her daughter. The very thought made her want to cry. She would do anything in the world for Sarah. That was why she'd moved back down here, after all, right into Lucas's firing-line. 'I'll make you a cup of tea,' she offered leadenly.

He reached into the bag and produced a half-gallon of milk in a plastic container. 'You'll need this if you do,' he said matter-of-factly.

'Oh, yes. Thank you.' She took it grudgingly, and turned to go into the kitchen. The milk was heavy. 'Just exactly how much did that bag weigh, Lucas?' she asked cagily.

He opened it to show her the stack of tinned food inside. 'Enough,' he said wryly, and she caught a hint of one of his taunting smiles.

'Then thank you again. You've gone to a lot of trouble for us.'

'For Sarah,' he said severely.

When she returned with two steaming mugs of tea he was sitting on the old sofa in front of the fire, his legs stretched out to the flickering flames, and his eyes closed.

She put the tea on the floor to the side of him, then crouched on the hearthrug in front of the blaze to warm herself through. There was a long silence. She felt horribly uncomfortable. He couldn't have fallen asleep, could he?

He hadn't. 'Look,' he said lazily at last, 'my legs are steaming.' She looked backwards over her shoulder. The wet denim was gently steaming in front of the fire.

'Are all your clothes damp?' she asked.

He nodded. 'Yes.'

'Oh, dear. I'm sorry. I haven't really got anything I can lend you for the journey back. I do have one enormous sweatshirt—but I don't think even that would fit.'

'That's OK,' he said casually, closing his eyes again. 'I shan't be going back tonight.'

Christie swivelled round. 'What? I mean—what about the horses...?'

'As you pointed out the last time I spent the night here, I pay people to tend to them these days. I may as well get my money's worth for once.'

'Oh. Yes. Even so...'

Lucas appeared to wake right up. He leaned forwards to the fire, resting his elbows on his knees and linking his hands between his splayed legs. 'Why don't we have a game of chess, Christie? I used to enjoy thrashing you at Percy's. It would help while away the evening—unless you're planning on taking a bath again.'

She deliberately chose to misunderstand him. 'There's no hot water left. I told you.'

'That didn't stop you the last time...'

Christie glowered at him. 'Let's not rake over old times, Lucas. I can hardly turf you out of the house in weather like this, but I don't much fancy having to spend the evening being belittled by you.'

'I wouldn't belittle your performance *that* evening, Christie. It was quite magnificent.'

'Well,' she said bitterly, *'you'd* know. You've performed in the company of enough prima donnas to make the comparison.'

Lucas laughed, a low, beguiling laugh. 'Whereas you are an innocent?' he queried sarcastically.

Christie squirmed. Why couldn't she fall out of love with the man? What was the matter with her? He was unfailingly unkind towards her. He made it plain that he despised her. For so long now she had felt that she deserved his harsh judgement. She had seduced him because...oh, dear...because she had been silly and innocent and hopelessly in love. For five years she had held fast to the certainty that Lucas could not be held to account. Everything that had happened was her own doing. She couldn't expect him to take any responsibility. He wasn't to blame in any way. Indeed, there was no reason in the world to stop loving him.

But lately things had changed. Lucas had *still* not asked. He still didn't want to know. It seemed to her that Lucas was choosing now, quite perversely, to continue to believe that Sarah was not his child. And in recent weeks she had found herself wanting him to question things, for Sarah's sake. The facts were there, dammit. All he had to do was confront them. She still acknowledged that she had been the orchestrator of her own destiny—she didn't want or expect any help from Lucas at all in bringing up her child. But when she saw how fond Sarah was becoming of him she felt angry and heartsore for the little girl. Lucas was her father. But he didn't want to know. Oh, she blamed him for that—she couldn't help herself. And yet still she loved him.

'I'll go upstairs and fetch the chess-board,' she said, making briskly for the hall. Thinking of Sarah was making her angry. She needed to get out of his presence to calm down.

'Close the door on the way out,' said Lucas drily. 'It's getting beautifully warm in here. Don't let all the heat out.'

She slammed the door hard behind her, hoping she was creating a chilling draught as she did so. 'I hope you freeze,' she muttered under her breath as she went.

When she came back downstairs she opened the door with a flourish, hoping to create in the air the very ice she was incapable of creating in her heart. But the sight which met her eyes had her closing the door very hurriedly behind her.

'Lucas! What if Sarah were to come down?'

'Am I not decent?' he asked, standing tall in front of the fire.

She gulped. He was still wearing his brief black underpants, so he had to be counted as decent. One saw such sights at the average swimming-pool every day of the week, after all, and she had no qualms about taking her daughter swimming. She closed her eyes. Except that...oh, no...one didn't see such sights at the average swimming-pool. Because none of the men there sent her pulses racing, and brought a hazy anticipation rushing to her skin, and a sharper, more focused pleasure to that dark place, deep inside her, which began to flood with raw desire.

Just a glimpse of his long, muscular form, the broad shoulders sloping gently away from his powerful neck, the angular jaw and the hard planes of his face, the flat, tanned abdomen, strewn with dark hairs which descended in a tapering line from his navel to the band of his dark briefs, had been enough to trip Christie's responses into overdrive. Even with her eyes closed she was becoming aroused. She could sense him all about her in the room. When she took in a breath her breasts seemed to surge against the fabric of her bra, her nipples prickling hard against the flimsy lace.

She opened her eyes again. He was leaning forward to adjust his damp clothes on the chairback near the fire. All the muscles in his chest rippled as he reached out first one powerful arm and then the other. Finally he lowered himself back on to the sofa. Now it was his legs which drew her eyes, bent squarely at the knee, his feet planted on the floor, his muscular thighs slightly apart. She looked away before he could catch her studying the play of firelight on his lightly tanned skin. But the fuzz of hairs on his calves dragged her eyes back to his legs, until her only defence was to lift a hand to shade her eyes.

'Where are you going to set out the board?' he asked, and she could tell from his voice that he was aware of the effect he was having on her, and was amused by her response.

'Lucas... put your clothes on,' she said plaintively, keeping her hand in front of her eyes, and turning her back on him.

'Do you want me to catch pneumonia?'

'No. Of course not. But really this is most... most...'

'You aren't *shocked*, are you, Christie? Good grief, you do surprise me.'

'I'm not shocked. Just uncomfortable.'

'Then come and sit on the rug in front of the fire and set up the pieces. You'll be quite comfy then.'

'That's not what I meant, and you know it.'

'Oh, stop playing the blushing virgin. It's very inappropriate. All I'm planning to do is beat you at chess. I shan't insist that you take your clothes off, too.'

'You mean just because I have a child I'm not allowed to be embarrassed at the sight of a half-naked man in my living-room?'

'I wasn't embarrassed when I came into this very room and found you *completely* naked. You could do me the favour of returning the compliment.'

'But you've had hundreds of girlfriends! I don't play in your league, Lucas. Anyway, I was embarrassed enough for us both.'

'Were you? Oh, yes, so you were at first. You got used to the idea quite quickly, though. You will this time, too. Now come on, there's a good girl. You can be white.'

She turned around and met his eye. 'Why are you doing this, Lucas?' she pleaded with a sigh.

His eyes flashed away from her face, alight with irritation. 'I'm doing it because I was damp and cold, and had nothing to change into in the morning. Unless I get my clothes dry in front of this blaze I shall be forced to hang around here until God knows what hour of the day, or walk miles back home in cold, wet clothes. It makes perfect sense to me. As I've saved you a muddy four-hour walk in the pouring rain with a grizzling child, I should think it would make perfect sense to you too. So stop being so bloody coy.'

Christie scowled at him. 'On the understanding that you leave at first light I'm prepared to accept the situation,' she conceded crossly.

Lucas slid down from the sofa and came to rest on the rug, his head leaning back on the seat, his knees bent. 'Excellent. We've agreed about something at last,' he said nastily.

Christie knelt down beside him and unfolded the chequered board, set out the carved pieces, and made her first move. All the while her body hummed with eager anticipation.

'Can't you alter the time switch on the water heater?' he asked, flicking a pawn forward with his thumb.

Christie kept her eyes fixed on the board. 'Yes,' she replied.

'Then why don't you? It must be very inconvenient having no hot water after a certain time in the day.'

'Inconvenient but economical,' she replied, moving out her queen's pawn.

'Are you really so penniless? I thought you had a good job.'

'I do. I'm a programmer for a very good agency. But I only work part-time. We're very far from being poor, but I have to watch the pennies none the less.'

'Doesn't Sarah's father contribute?'

'No.' Oh, God... Why wasn't it as obvious to him as it was to everyone else in the village that Sarah couldn't have been conceived before the summer holidays? She was *his*. It was as plain as the nose on his face.

'Take back that move.'

'Why?'

'It was just plain stupid. I want to win—but not that fast.'

Christie changed her move. 'Better?' she snapped.

'Oh, much. That's a much more interesting proposition... Why not?'

'Why not what?'

'Why doesn't he contribute?'

Christie swallowed hard. 'He... he doesn't know that I have a child,' she said.

'He does, you know.'

Her eyes skittered upwards and met his. There was a crooked, knowing smile on his face, and his eyes were half hooded, challenging. Oh, lord. So he *did* realise that Sarah was his child...

'What do you mean?' she asked guardedly, her mouth suddenly dry with fear.

'James Lakey... That's his name, isn't it? He knows you have a child. He told a friend of mine—do you remember Lisa? Anyway, she's a sort of second cousin of his and she sees his family when she's in London. Anyway, he told her and she repeated it back to me...'

'Does he?' she asked airily, suddenly light-headed with a mixture of relief and anger. Why was he being so perversely dense? Perversity was Lucas's style. But density...? He liked Sarah now that he'd met her. You'd think he'd be proud to acknowledge such a sweet child as his own.

'Well, that's not so surprising,' she continued stiffly. 'He was at Braizeneath, and as Dad still teaches there and I take Sarah to visit quite often it must be common knowledge among the old pupils. But he doesn't know that he's... he's the father.'

'Surely he must have guessed?'

'Er—well, I couldn't say, actually...' Her voice sounded rather faint, even to her own ears.

'Christie, do you think I'm completely stupid? Do you think I can't count?'

'What?' Christie almost jumped out of her skin. He *knew*. He was going to say something. If he asked now she'd deny it. Deny it until she was blue in the face...

'Look. You move your knight out there, and then I do that... One... two... three moves and you have to resign...'

Except that it wouldn't be fair on Sarah if she denied it. If Lucas refused to acknowledge her, that was one thing. But did she have the right to deny her child access to her own father if that was what he wanted?

'Count?' she breathed.

'The moves. Look at the board.'

'Oh. Sorry, Lucas. I wasn't concentrating.'

'What the hell is the matter with you this evening?'

'Nothing,' she replied sullenly, locking her eyes on to the meaningless jumble of pieces on the board.

'Is it the sight of my naked torso, Christie?' he teased. 'Is that what's putting you off your game?'

'Yes,' she said hastily, anxious not to have him guess the truth. Then, realising that she had just as good as admitted that his presence was arousing her, she looked up wildly. 'No. Oh, I don't know. I just feel very uncomfortable with you sitting here so...so...'

He threw back his head and laughed. 'Shall I make you feel comfortable? Huh?'

'No! Of course not. Anyway, you said... I mean, we agreed not to make the same mistake...'

'I know. But I have to admit that whatever I think of you, Christie, the mere memory of your passionate lovemaking could make me overcome my scruples at the drop of a hat.'

'Your scruples!' she exclaimed, suddenly furious with him. He might want her, but he didn't want his own child! 'You don't have any scruples, Lucas! Oh, why did you have to come here tonight? We were fine, Sarah and I, we were fine! We don't need your help. I can look after my daughter by myself! Oh, why did you have to come here?' She could feel her eyes fill with hot tears of rage. And why, oh, why did she still want him so much?

CHAPTER SEVEN

AND then Lucas did something very surprising, and utterly disarming. He reached forward and brushed her hair back from her eyes very tenderly and very gently. He drew the side of his thumb across her temple and then let his hand drop. She hugged herself tight, kneeling in front of him, quivering at the unexpected sensitivity of his touch.

'Don't be angry with *me*, Christie,' he said softly. 'I know how hard these past years must have been for you. I wouldn't have interfered, but Sarah was premature. I can't help being concerned that she might still be a little delicate. That's why I wanted to air the house for you back in May. And it's why I wanted to make sure you were all right this evening.'

Christie looked at him with an expression of pained shock in her eyes. He had actually spelled out the fact that he knew when his daughter had been due! Quite unconsciously she began to wring her hands in response to the dismay which thickened, like a grey fog, inside her.

So how could he go on believing that she was Lakey's child, when he knew perfectly well that she hadn't seen Lakey since before the summer holiday had begun? Oh, she'd always been conscious that he *must* have known when the baby was due, because her aunt had been so thrilled and had broadcast the news so widely, but she'd managed to half convince herself there had been some misunderstanding and that he'd got things wrong. And yet now he was admitting that he knew perfectly well that Sarah had been due *exactly* nine months after the night of the party.

When Sarah had just been a nameless child, an inconvenient, runny-nosed product of his imagination, far away in London, it might have been understandable. But he saw Sarah every day now. He chatted with her and went out of his way to see her because he liked her. Now that she was real to him, didn't he have the courage to own that she was his? It wasn't as if Christie had ever tried to make any demands on him—he surely couldn't think that she wanted anything from him. The only thing she wanted was to be able to tell her child that she had a father—just like everybody else.

Christie's anger began to solidify, until it was a hard, cold thing, lodged firmly beneath her heart. 'Delicate?' she challenged bitterly. 'She's as strong as an ox.'

Lucas grimaced. 'Feel angry with *him*,' he continued soothingly. 'He's been a bastard. He must know. It must be obvious to him. He should have stood by you when she arrived early and was ill.'

Christie almost exploded with fury. 'Obvious? She was ten *days* early, Lucas, not ten weeks. And she wasn't really *ill* at all—just slow to feed. They took her to the special-care unit for twenty-four hours because I'd had a hard time and I was exhausted. She's a perfectly healthy child and I'm a perfectly good mother. I don't need *anyone's* help in bringing her up.'

There was a long silence. Lucas's keen auburn eyes seemed almost black as they stared out of his face. Then the creases beneath his eyes sharpened as his eyes narrowed and his mouth hardened into a thin line. Even the grooves in his face deepened and darkened. 'Ten days early?' His voice snagged, as if it were being dragged over barbed wire.

Christie looked back at him, her features pale and set. She was too angry to care about her precious vow of silence any longer. 'So you've done your sums at last...' she muttered scornfully. 'What took you so long?'

Lucas tipped himself on to his feet, crouching in front of her, and grabbed hold of her shoulders with a fierce intensity. 'Christie. She's *my* child. My God—how could you have lied to me? How could you?'

Christie tried to pull back, but he was holding on to her too hard. 'You've been lying to *yourself*,' she bit out between clenched teeth.

He shook his head. 'You told me she wasn't mine... It was a lie.'

The accusation wounded her. Of course he was right—but, even so, he'd had a long time to work out the truth. She resented the implication that she was entirely at fault.

'I...I didn't exactly lie—or not in the way you mean. You see...well, it's complicated, but I *did* think I was having James Lakey's child. For a little while.'

About five or six hours at the most, she acknowledged with an irritable sigh.

'But you must have known once you saw a doctor. They do scans and things these days. They don't get muddled over dates like they used to.'

She stared furiously into the fire. 'Yes. I knew then.'

'So why didn't you tell me?'

'Because you wanted me to have the baby adopted. What would have been the point?'

His hands dropped to his side. His face was set in hard, unyielding lines. 'My God. Sarah is my child,' he said quietly. And then his face twisted into a bitter, sardonic smile. 'So when shall we get married, Christie?'

'Don't be so stupid,' she managed to stutter.

'You *will* marry me, Christie,' he affirmed mockingly.

A jagged scribble of pain coloured the space behind her eyes. Abruptly her face crumpled with emotion. Oh... All the years she had dreamed of him saying those words... All the long, weary years... And now he was taunting her with it. It was more than she could bear. She closed her eyes. The tears squeezed out from the corners and trickled down her nose.

His arms came around her, tight, ruthlessly, like a cruel band of steel as he pulled her harshly against him. 'Better late than never,' he muttered acridly, his mouth close to her ear. 'You'll have to marry me, Christie. For Sarah's sake if nothing else.'

Then the sobbing began in earnest. She lurched wretchedly against his bare skin. Her mouth opened to let out the muffled moans, and she felt the skin of his shoulder, salty with tears, yield against her teeth. She tried to shake her head, but he held her too firmly.

'Yes,' he said. 'I won't have it any other way.'

She rubbed her hot forehead against his collarbone.

'No. I don't want to marry you. I never wanted that.'

'Well, it's what you're going to get, whether you like it or not. You told me she wasn't mine and I believed you. But you've let the truth come out now and there's no going back. Sarah's my child and I intend making her mine.'

'Let go of me, Lucas.'

'For God's sake, why? You're my... fiancée. You're upset. I shall hold you until you stop crying. Isn't that the way it should be, Christie?' There was a callous cynicism driving his words.

Oh, lord. What was she to do? She loved this man with every last scrap of her being. There was no other man she would ever want or ever wed. And he was holding her close and even now she could taste the maleness of him on her tongue and hear her flesh cry out to him. How could she refuse him?

'I'm not your fiancée. And I don't want you to touch me. Let me go.'

If only he would let her go she would be able to think straight. Crushed against his naked torso, she was being weakened by the aching poignancy of her desire.

Slowly, contemptuously, he let his arms drop away. She shuffled sideways, and came to rest some feet away from him, hunched on the hearthrug, hugging her knees. But the power of his presence filled the air between them. It made no difference at all that he wasn't holding her any more. She was every bit as aware of him as she had been before. She still yearned to succumb.

'Well, Christie? Do you concede defeat? Checkmate?'

Oh, yes. She conceded defeat. But she prayed that her acquiescence could be laid at Sarah's door—not her own. Let it be for her child's sake that she was saying yes. For if she had to live with the knowledge that it was her own craven need that had driven her to the decision she would despise herself forever. She would marry him for Sarah's sake alone. Lucas had learned that there was at least one child on the face of this earth who could stir his affection—and, as fate would have it, she was *his* child. The time had arrived for Lucas to take a wife. Canon Percival hadn't been able to persuade him, but little Sarah had. And so Christie would have to be that wife.

'Can't you give me a few days to think, Lucas?'

'No. What is there to think about?'

He was right. How *could* she refuse him? What would be the point? He was Sarah's father, and Sarah already loved him, though she was far too young to put it into words.

'Checkmate...' she said woodenly.

He reached out a single finger and with it turned her tear-blotched face to his. He looked at her very seriously, and then a swift, crooked smile danced at one corner of his mouth. 'Would you like to seal that with a kiss?' he asked.

She groaned inwardly. That smile... it was irresistible... and yet this time she *would* resist. If she let him kiss her, then they'd surely end up making love. And just now the last thing she wanted was for him to see how much his body moved her. She had betrayed her promise to herself—she had forced him to ask the very question he had not wanted to ask, and had as good as forced him into marriage. If they made love now with her defences so low he would glimpse her love. He would know that she had loved him even then, and would feel that she had trapped him, and their child would be the loser.

Instead she wanted him to feel that he had been trapped by a little child's bright eyes—which was, after all, the truth... and perhaps just as it should be. He was her father; she was his daughter. Sarah might have captured him, but at least the innocent little girl would never harness his free spirit with bitterness.

She shook her head. 'No, Lucas. Not now,' she said wearily. 'I think I'll go to bed. You can sleep in the spare room—the bed's made up. But don't touch any of the computer stuff in there, will you?'

She washed her face in cold water and cleaned her teeth. Then she curled up in the high old bed in the narrow room and listened to the rain. Her eyes felt gritty and heavy, but she couldn't sleep. Nor could she cry.

She heard Lucas moving about the house. It grew very late. Still he didn't come upstairs. She dozed intermittently, but kept waking with a start. The rain poured from the gutters in a steady stream. The wind buffeted the trees behind the house so that they creaked and rattled. At last she heard Lucas's soft footfalls on the staircase, and then froze as the door to her room eased open.

'Christie?'

She closed her eyes and pretended to be asleep. He came into the room and closed the door behind him.

'Christie? Wake up...'

She pretended to stir. 'What is it?' she mumbled, then, suddenly more alert, said anxiously, 'Is it the water? Is it coming in the house?'

'Nothing like that.'

'Oh. Good.'

'Move over. I'm going to share your bed.'

'No!'

'Yes. I shan't kiss you or ask you to make love with me. But we're going to be married, Christie. We shall be sharing a bed then. It will be easier if we start tonight.'

'But Lucas, I really don't think I can handle it.'

He sat heavily on the side of the bed and laid his hand on her hip. 'It's better this way, Christie. We'll have to sleep together from the start once we're married. I want everything to seem right in Sarah's eyes. But I don't think I could quite manage the age-old ritual of carrying you over the threshold like a virgin bride on our wedding night in the circumstances. Let's just get on with it, eh? I promise I shan't ask you to make love until you feel ready for it.'

'Oh.' She rolled over so that she was close to the wall, her back to him. He was right. It would be too embarrassing to have to go through some sort of fake wedding night with a man who didn't love her and who didn't really want to be married to her. It would be easier for him to start getting used to the situation as soon as possible.

He came into the bed beside her.

'You're freezing!' she whispered.

'The fire's died back,' he said wryly. 'But you're beautifully warm, Christie.'

'Oh, I know *everything* there is to know about keeping warm in bed,' she returned sarcastically.

He laughed his warm, melodic laugh, and then laid one cold arm in the hollow of her waist, the pad of his thumb wriggling under the waistband of her pyjama trousers to rest in her navel.

She shuddered.

'I'll warm up in a minute,' he murmured.

Christie swallowed hard. She hadn't been shivering because he was cold. She didn't reply.

'I meant what I said...' he continued reassuringly. 'I shan't kiss you until you make it quite plain that you want me to.'

If only he knew! She wanted nothing more than to turn to him in the dark and feel his hot mouth cover hers. She curled into an even tighter ball and closed her eyes. For long minutes she was burningly aware of him, virtually naked beside her. But the temptation to turn towards him and invite his passion slowly seeped away. He didn't want her as his wife—not really—not in the way a man should want a woman. He would dutifully make love to her when the time came. He found her desirable, so perhaps it wouldn't be such a hard penance after all. But she wouldn't force it on him yet. Certainly not tonight. This night he felt nothing but bitterness towards her. Exhausted and drained, she sank gently into sleep.

She woke once in the night. Lucas was warm and relaxed beside her, his breathing deep and regular. One long, muscular arm still lay across her, and if she kept her eyes closed and didn't allow herself to think she could imagine that his arm held her with all the pride of possession that a man should feel for the woman he was about to marry. It seemed that she was to have her heart's desire, after all. More than anything now she wanted Lucas to have his.

The room was unexpectedly silent when she awoke the following morning. She was alone in the bed. She reached out and flicked back the curtain. A soft drizzle hung like a mist in the air, but the fierce downpour had stopped.

She heard Sarah's stomping footsteps coming upstairs, followed by Lucas's more steady ones. The bedroom door burst open, and Sarah rushed in followed by Lucas, bearing a breakfast tray and smiling wickedly.

'Mummy! Guess what!'

Christie sat up, and pushed her thick, tousled hair back from her eyes. 'What, darling?' She kept her eyes fixed on her daughter, embarrassed to have Lucas see her looking so early-morningish.

Sarah looked uncertainly at Lucas and said, 'I can tell her, can't I? It's not a secret?'

'You can tell her,' he said solemnly.

Sarah clambered up on to the bed, and patted her mother's hair tenderly with her fat little hand. 'Well, Soloman is going to be my pony.'

'Tell her the rest,' prompted Lucas, obviously trying hard not to laugh.

Sarah screwed up her face with the effort of recalling the more trivial details of her important news. Then enlightenment dawned. 'Oh, yes. I remember now. Lucas is going to be my daddy. It means you've got to marry him, I think. Can I be bridesmaid and have a dress and ride on Soloman?'

'Oh... well, if you want to.' Then she smiled lovingly at her daughter and added, 'Are you happy, darling?'

Sarah nodded. 'Oh, yes. He's a bit big. But I'll get used to him.'

'Who? Lucas?'

'Don't be silly. Soloman. Can I have white, pointy shoes like we saw that time and you said weren't suitable?'

Lucas sat on the end of the bed and reached out to take Sarah's hand. 'We'll have to get you a proper riding hat and breeches and boots as well, and we'll have a marriage picnic in the stables with apples for all the horses.'

Sarah beamed and clapped her hands with delight. Christie looked down at her own hands. He had obviously decided exactly how it was going to be. She hadn't been consulted. But then, she supposed, she had forgone her right to choose for herself a long time ago.

'Sound all right to you, Christie?' asked Lucas.

Christie looked at him in surprise. There had been no hint of sarcasm in his voice. Clearly he had meant what he said last night about making it all seem right for Sarah. While they had the little girl's attention she was going to be safe from the lacerations of his tongue.

'Yes,' she said numbly. 'Fine.'

Lucas handed her the breakfast tray. 'Eat up. There's plenty of hot water. I'll draw you a bath as soon as you've finished. Then we can discuss our plans for the day.'

Christie looked down at the familiar old tray with its wickerwork handles. The wicker had been unravelling for as long as she could remember. Now it had been expertly whipped into order with a length of string.

'You've mended the tray,' she said.

'Is that all you can say?' he admonished.

'Thank you for the rose,' she added huskily. 'It's beautiful.'

Lucas's eyes glittered, and his mouth curled into a thin smile. 'I'm glad you like it. I've lit the fire and cleaned up behind me in the kitchen, too. Do you think I have the makings of a good husband?'

'A good husband?' she echoed incredulously. 'I've never thought of you that way at all, Lucas!'

His eyes turned to look out of the window. 'Any more than I can imagine you as a good wife...' he murmured drily. 'But look, I even warmed the pot before I made the tea. Now what do you think of that?'

'How many shelves have you put up?' she returned with mock-severity, glad of the invitation to treat his question lightly. She hadn't trusted her voice when she had thanked him for the rose. She dared not give herself away.

He shrugged benignly. 'Eat that egg before it hatches,' he said briskly. 'I'm taking Sarah outside. We'll see if we can catch a fish for lunch.'

While Christie tackled her breakfast she could hear the water gushing into the bath. By the time she was ready to go into the bathroom Lucas's and Sarah's voices could be heard outside. Lucas was clearly very happy to be gaining a daughter. She could guess how he felt about gaining a wife, though, but at least he was taking great pains to do the right thing. Perhaps it would be all right, after all.

He stayed all day. He could easily have made it back to Home Farm on foot, especially once the rain started to ease off a little. But whenever she urged him to go he frowned coldly and she felt guilty. Obviously he wanted to spend as much time with his daughter as possible, and she didn't feel as if she had the right to make him go. He was delightful with Sarah, teasing and making her laugh one minute, then gently reproving her when her excitement made her over-exuberant. Christie hovered in the background, feeling like a spare part.

'Why don't you sit down and read?' he asked her at one point.

'No. It's OK...'

'I'd have gone for the papers if only I'd had a boat. Still, don't you have a book?'

'No.'

'What about a nap, then?'

'I'm not tired.'

Lucas sighed. 'Well, do a crossword. There's a pile of old newspapers in the pantry. There must be a crossword you can do in one of them.'

Did he actually remember that she used to be a crossword addict? Or had he just said it by chance? It didn't really matter. Either way, it couldn't be more obvious that he didn't want her company. 'I don't do them any more,' she said quietly.

She wandered off into the kitchen and made a cup of coffee. She really ought to be feeling more pleased that Lucas and Sarah were getting on so well, instead of which she felt hurt and resentful and left out. She was in danger of saying something unkind. It wouldn't do. He was behaving impeccably. She was going to be his wife no matter what. She would have to learn to get used to the situation if she was to ensure his happiness. When she took the coffee through she was wearing a bright smile. Sarah was sitting cross-legged in front of the television, watching a programme for the under-fives.

'Would you mind if I went upstairs and got on with some work?' she asked lightly.

One corner of Lucas's mouth tightened with irritation. 'You don't need to work now, Christie,' he said. 'Or hasn't last night's conversation sunk in properly.'

'Er—I have to admit I hadn't really thought as far as to what was going to happen about my work. But we aren't married yet, and in the meantime I've got a lot I ought to be getting on with.'

'Why?'

'Because I'm under contract—and anyway, I owe it to the agency. Steven has given me the most interesting jobs and has made sure I haven't run short of work for four years now. Whatever happens, I owe it to him to complete my current assignment efficiently.'

'So you feel under some sort of obligation to this...Steven...?' muttered Lucas, clearly annoyed.

'Why shouldn't I?'

'That's a very good question... Might I suggest you're better fitted to answer it than I am?'

She looked at him blankly for a moment, before dawning realisation brought a high colour to her heart-shaped face. Her assertion back in May that she'd had a steady stream of lovers had left its mark, even though she'd amended it later. She glanced across at Sarah. The little girl was engrossed her programme, but even so she couldn't risk saying too much right now.

'I don't know if there's a sort of casting couch for computer programmers,' she replied quietly, 'but if there is I can assure you I've never encountered it. Steven has kept me generously supplied with work because he knew my circumstances.'

'Well, lucky old Steven,' said Lucas so sourly that Christie turned on her heel and stalked off upstairs before she said something she might regret.

Later, when they were alone, she would try again to undo the damage she had done by implying that she was West Ealing's most notorious *femme fatale*. It was her own fault, as usual, but she couldn't let him go on believing something like *that*.

She spent the rest of the day concentrating hard on her work. The sooner she got this program completed, the better. Anyway, she was glad of the distraction. Lucas and Sarah were having a fine time. The little girl hadn't come looking for her mother once. Christie wasn't jealous—how could she be? But she felt painfully isolated.

At about five Lucas came looking for her. He stuck his head around the door and gave one of his wry smiles. Her heart screeched to a halt. Oh, lord... Just the sight of his face turned her bones to water. How was she going to survive being married to him for the rest of her life without giving herself away completely?

'I've got to go back to Home Farm for a while. I've some calls I have to make.'

She let out a sigh of relief. 'Oh. That's fine. I quite understand. You've given us a lot of your time already.'

Lucas's eyes flashed darkly. 'I shall be giving you the rest of my life,' he said bitterly. 'There's no need to protest your gratitude just for one day. I'll be back to sleep here.'

Christie fixed her eyes on the screen. So he thought she should be grateful for his offer of marriage? She was too hurt to reply.

She went to bed very early, and feigned sleep when she heard Lucas arrive. When he slipped under the covers beside her she was tight against her side of the bed, breathing deeply. She went on pretending to sleep for hours and hours, while her body was more awake than it had ever been. It was no easier the next night, nor the next. She still didn't trust herself not to let her love show in the face of such overpowering desire. He kept up the pattern for a week. He came to the cottage during the day while Sarah was about, and then returned to Home Farm for long stretches to work. But every night he slept in Christie's bed, and every night she turned her back and screwed her eyes tight shut and scolded her treacherous body for wanting him so much.

The following Monday he stayed all day. He interrupted her at her work a little before four-thirty.

'Come on,' he said. 'I've packed your things. We're off.'

'Off where?'

'Home. My place. There's no point in staying here now. At last the flood water's completely disappeared.'

'But...' She sighed. But what? Lucas called the shots now. Greyly she switched off the computer and followed him downstairs.

The air was damp outside, but there was no trace of rain, and the grey sky had a light yellow band shivering above the horizon to remind them of the sun. The mud everywhere was heavy and clinging. Steadily they trudged in their wellingtons through the gate and up the sloping field beyond.

Sarah danced ahead, her little red boots bright against the soaking grass. Lucas had his packed holdall slung over one shoulder. Christie stuffed her hands in her pockets, and breathed in the raw autumnal air. She looked up at him. He hadn't shaved. His chin was dark with a day's growth of heavy beard. His hair fell across his forehead. She looked hastily away, but in her mind's eye she could still see him with outstanding clarity. And then she seemed to be standing at a distance, watching them from afar. The man, the woman and the child, walking away from one life and into another. Lucas was walking with a confident air, his chin up, his footsteps strong. Sarah skipped happily ahead, as if she couldn't wait. Only her own footsteps faltered. She looked at the brow of the hill and consciously straightened her back. She took her hands out of her jacket pockets and let her arms fall relaxed and easy at her side. She had weathered the past five years cheerfully. She wasn't going to let the next fifty defeat her.

'Lucas?' she said determinedly.

'Yes?'

'That conversation back in May, when I claimed to have lots of boyfriends?'

He stopped walking and drew in a sharp breath, looking down on her scornfully. 'Look, Christie, your past, sordid or otherwise, is out of bounds as a topic of conversation from now on. I'd be grateful if you'd bear that in mind.'

'But the thing is, Lucas, really, I didn't give you a very——'

'Shut up, Christie.'

'Lucas! I can't go on letting you believe something like that.'

The expression of disdain deepened. 'Christie,' he said coldly, 'I don't give a damn what you want me to believe. I shall exercise my own judgement—in everything. From now on you are going to behave like a good wife—whether you like it or not. What's past, unfortunately, is beyond remedy. You've committed yourself to this marriage. For Sarah's sake I don't intend letting you either back out of it, or renege on your vows once the ceremony is over. You owe me that. In return I shall be a good provider, and a good father. If you have any objections you'd better register them in writing, because I'm damned if I'll listen to another word on the subject.' And with that he started walking again.

Christie stared at him, shocked. He looked so unremittingly severe. He clearly meant every word. She dared not say anything further. What was the point in antagonising him, anyway? She had forced him into this situation. It was no good complaining that modern marriages were based on equality and sharing. Modern marriages were also based on love. If she had wanted a husband who loved her she should have accepted all those offers of dates, long, long ago. She had turned her back on every other man in the world except Lucas, and now she had to live with the consequences.

CHAPTER EIGHT

LUCAS, Christie and Sarah were greeted on their arrival by the housekeeper, Mrs Grey, and a blushing, grinning Janine, who revealed that Lucas had asked her to come and live in for the next few months as a temporary nanny. The girl was obviously delighted to have a 'proper' job, and thanked Lucas effusively before whisking Sarah off excitedly to show her the house.

'I think I'll go with them,' murmured Christie, feeling suddenly shy and longing for Janine's easy company. 'I'd like to see around.'

But Lucas laid a hand circumspectly on her arm. 'I'll show you the house later. Come through to the sitting-room and have a drink before dinner.'

The farmhouse had been wonderfully transformed, incorporating an adjoining barn seamlessly into the structure, so that the main living-room was exceptionally large, surrounded by a gallery which led to rooms on the upper floor. It was comfortably furnished with traditional English furniture—mostly antiques—and huge oriental rugs, which brought moments of subtle, rich colour to the restful interior.

'It's beautiful,' said Christie, quite awestruck at the realisation that this was to be her home. She looked around her anxiously. The house that she had visited when it had belonged to Reg and Lily Crabtree bore no resemblance to this spacious residence. It made her feel even more guilty at the idea that she had somehow 'trapped' Lucas.

'It must have cost a fortune to convert the barn...' she blurted out ingenuously.

Lucas shrugged. 'A fair bit. But the basic structure of the house was good and it was all very well proportioned, so it wasn't difficult. Now come and sit down and tell me what you'd like to drink.'

Christie wandered across to a chintz sofa positioned close to the wide ingle-nook and perched on the edge. 'I'll have a—er—a tomato juice, thank you.'

Lucas opened the age-blackened doors of a carved Jacobean cupboard and extracted a couple of glasses and some bottles. He poured himself a finger of Scotch before opening her little bottle of tomato juice. 'You like this stuff, do you?'

'Er—yes. Thank you. It's very nice.'

Lucas shook his head impatiently. 'What I mean is, do you drink it regularly? Bloody Marys or what?'

She looked at him blankly. 'Oh. No. Not really.'

He sighed. 'It's just that this is your home now, Christie. This cupboard's pretty well stocked, but I'll make sure we get in plenty of whatever it is you drink.'

'Oh. I see. Yes. Thank you.'

'So a couple of bottles of vodka would be a good idea?'

'Oh. If you like. Yes. I don't think I've ever tasted it, but it's supposed to be very nice.'

Lucas sighed more forcefully. 'So what *do* you usually drink?' he persisted.

Christie shrugged. 'Nothing much. White wine, usually. I think.'

Lucas handed her her glass with an air of distinct annoyance and came to sit opposite her. He stuck out his legs aggressively and leaned his head back in the chair. He closed his eyes.

Christie felt like weeping. She felt so shy and awkward, sitting there sipping at her drink. Lucas seemed so much at home here—well, that was hardly surprising—but it rubbed in the fact that she was a complete outsider... and suddenly she felt as if she didn't know him at all. The Lucas she had known all those years ago hadn't had a home like this, for a start.

'This house isn't a bit like your parents',' she commented weakly.

'Thank God,' he muttered, his eyes still closed. 'Gloomy old museum of a place. It hasn't been decorated in years.'

'But I thought that was because...' she cut herself short.

'Because what?'

'Nothing.'

He pulled a bored, disdainful face, opening his eyes and regarding her balefully. 'Oh, come on, Christie. Spit it out.'

She blushed. 'What I was about to say,' she explained crossly, 'was based on village gossip. Being your...fiancée is going to take some getting used to in the circumstances.'

Lucas looked away. 'It certainly is if you're going to persist in your ambition to turn into the speaking clock. You were going to say that my parents haven't redecorated for years because they're too mean. Weren't you?'

'No,' she said. Then drawing courage from his insult, added, 'As it happens, I was going to say that it was because they were too poor. Rumour always had it that they'd lost a lot of money.'

Lucas let out a short laugh. 'They did. But I took over the day-to-day running of the place as soon as I'd left school. And, as I'd been managing my own small portfolio since I was thirteen, I already had a fair amount of experience to fall back on. Their fortunes have been restored for well over a decade now. As it happens, the reason that they *don't* redecorate is because they are indeed too mean.'

Christie leaned forward in her chair, suddenly feeling a good deal less shy. 'Why did you come back here to live, Lucas? You always swore blind that you were leaving just as soon as you were old enough. It was common knowledge.'

Lucas closed his eyes again. The tip of his tongue appeared between his lips. 'I came back because I discovered that there's more than one way to skin a cat...' he said cryptically. Then he added more thoughtfully, 'I liked this place. I liked the horses and the land—and even the sense of history—up to a point. But I didn't see eye to eye with my father, nor with his way of running things. When I was very young I thought that running away was an answer. However, it dawned on me that the remedy lay in my own hands. When I should have been studying Latin, I was reading up on farming and livestock management and business practice. I began following the stock market. I looked into the idea of new rural enterprises. And then, when I knew how I wanted to handle it, I simply made up my mind to take over and do things my way. It's all worked out just as I hoped.' There was a brief pause, then he said slowly, 'In more ways than you could imagine.'

'Oh, I'd heard about the saw mill and the furniture factory and that place where they grow and package herbs.'

'That wasn't what I meant,' he returned coolly.

'Oh.' Christie sighed. Was this how their conversations were going to be for the next fifty years? 'You certainly took everyone around here by surprise,' she ventured brightly.

'Did I? Well, let's see how surprised they are by this latest step in my career... I'm sure our marriage will cause more than a little comment.'

Christie was disconcerted by the remark. She could quite well imagine what people would say and think. Still, she'd claimed to be proud to hold her head up in this small community. Let them say what they liked... She wasn't going to let anyone change that. 'What happened to make you change your mind about coming back here, Lucas?' she asked, anxious to change the subject.

Lucas sighed impatiently. 'Percy,' he said. 'Speaking of whom... we'll be seeing him first thing tomorrow.'

'To discuss the wedding plans?' she asked, suddenly nervous again.

'No. I did that on the phone the other night. We'll be seeing him tomorrow because he'll be officiating at our wedding.'

Christie only just managed to restrain herself from jumping to her feet. 'Tomorrow?' she exclaimed. 'But we can't!'

'Why not? There isn't something you'd like to tell me, is there, Christie? I mean, you're not married already or anything, are you?'

'Of course not!'

'Then what's the problem? Why wait?'

She looked at him, wide-eyed with dismay. His eyes were *still* closed. 'Because...' She ran her tongue over her lips. 'Because we don't know each other, Lucas!' she said firmly.

'On the contrary. I would have said we know exactly as much as we need to know about one another to qualify us for that short walk to the altar.'

'Lucas!' Her voice was husky with pleading.

He opened his dark eyes wide and tilted his chin and smiled. 'What's the problem, Christie? You aren't going to back out.' He said it as if it was a statement, not a question.

'I...' She cast her mind around desperately. They were getting married in the morning and he didn't even know what she liked to drink, and she felt like a day-tripper at a stately home in his house, and it was all...oh, it was all *impossible*.

'Yesterday,' she said fiercely, 'yesterday I was a working woman with a child of four and a house of my own and I was in control of my own life. I worked very hard for all of that, Lucas. You're treating me as if none of it counts.'

Now it was Lucas's turn to sigh. 'You can get used to all the changes *after* we're married, can't you? It's no reason for delaying things.'

'Yes, but...but I haven't anything to wear.'

He shrugged. 'I've sorted that out. And in case you're wondering, I haven't arranged a marquee on the lawn and invited a thousand guests. It'll just be the two of us.'

'Oh.'

There was a long silence. Lucas reached into a magazine rack near his chair and extracted a neatly folded newspaper. He glanced at it briefly and then put it down. 'If you'll excuse me...' he said tiredly, getting to his feet. 'I have a few things to see to. Make yourself at home.'

She sat perched on the edge of her chair for nearly half an hour, feeling anything but at home. The place smelt foreign, for a start. Oh, it was a nice smell of polish and fresh flowers, but it didn't smell like home.

At last Lucas sauntered back into the room. He rubbed one hand over his stubbly chin. 'Now if you don't mind I think I'll go and take a bath...' he said.

Christie swallowed hard. 'Right. If you could just point me in the direction of the kitchen I'll get a little supper for Sarah and put her to bed.'

Lucas shook his head slowly. 'No need. Janine's fed her and I've just put her to bed.'

'Oh.' Christie blinked hard. She had always put Sarah to bed—except for that time back in May when she'd stayed with the aunts, but that was different. 'Perhaps I'll just go and find her and make sure she's all right and read her a story,' she said anxiously.

But Lucas shook his head decisively again. 'No. I've read her a story and she's drifting off to sleep. She's fine. Anyway, Janine will fetch you if she cries for you.'

'I know, but——'

'But nothing. You can come upstairs with me. I'll show you our room. You can take a bath too. There are several bathrooms—although you could always join me...'

'Lucas!' She felt her face colour hotly.

He laughed. 'It's your decision, Christie. I shan't press the point. But you can come on up with me and get changed, anyway.'

'I... I'll wait until you've finished,' she said.

'Why?'

'We're not alone in the house,' Christie muttered stiffly.

'Are you embarrassed about what the staff will think? Good lord, Christie, we're going to be married in the morning!'

'I know. But we aren't married yet,' she spat.

He raised his eyebrows and his auburn eyes glittered. 'You didn't let that stop you before...' he taunted. 'But then we were alone on the premises—on both occasions. Do you really care so much what other people think?'

'Lucas, you don't understand. It's all right for you. You've never cared one jot about what anybody thought. It's always been your style to do exactly what you wanted without giving a thought to the consequences. But I'm...different.'

He put one arm firmly around her shoulder. 'No, you're not,' he said scathingly and began to lead her towards the staircase and up to the gallery.

Completely at a loss, she allowed herself to be led. Once they were in his—their—luxurious bedroom she ducked out from under his arm and sat tentatively on the edge of the enormous bed. Sitting neatly on a hanger, hooked to the outside of an elegant mirror-fronted wardrobe, was one of her cotton print skirts and a clean pink T-shirt. Lucas had clearly thought of everything. As had Mrs Grey. They had been freshly ironed, ready for her to put on.

'Did Mrs Grey put those clothes there?' she asked.

Lucas nodded, kicking off his shoes and tugging his sweater over his head.

Christie sighed. Well, if Mrs Grey was so used to Lucas having ladies in his bedroom that she actually set out their clothes for them, it was a bit foolish of her to get so het up about what the woman might think. Anyway, she acknowledged ruefully, Mrs Grey's opinion had only played a small part in her reluctance to come upstairs with him. Mainly she had been frightened of witnessing exactly what she was witnessing now...which was Lucas undressing right in front of her eyes. He had half turned away from her, and was unbuttoning his shirt and looking toward the black, uncurtained window which threw his own reflection back at him. Flustered, she got to her feet and pulled the curtains before scuttling back to the bed.

He had undone the collar and cuffs and most of the buttons down the front, and was easing the shirt-tails out of the waistband of his jeans. She wanted to look away, but her eyes were transfixed by the sight of his broad chest gradually being revealed. Any minute now he would throw off his shirt and step out of his trousers and she would see that line of hairs disappearing into the black briefs...

She dragged her eyes away and determinedly turned her head to look over her shoulder. She found herself surveying an expanse of ecru lace counterpane, stretched neatly over mounds of soft pillows. Their bed. She would be sharing this bed with him just a few hours from now. She began to nibble worriedly at the tip of one thumb. So far she had managed to turn away from Lucas and go to sleep, because she hadn't wanted him to see how much she loved him. She had vaguely assumed that she would refuse to make love until she felt she had her feelings firmly under control. But then she had also assumed that it would be a little while before they got married. What was it he had said? He couldn't bear the idea of carrying her over the threshold like a virgin bride? Oh, dear. Tomorrow would be their wedding night. Unless she could bring herself to invite his passion tonight, she was going to have a horrible situation to face the following evening. They'd be married, and she would either walk across the threshold of their bedroom alone, her library book in one hand, a mug of cocoa in the other, and her winceyette pyjamas tucked under the pillow waiting for her... or... or they would have to endure exactly the sort of fake wedding night he wanted to avoid.

She was being carried along by a momentum she couldn't control. If he was to be spared that, then they would have to make love tonight, and she wasn't yet ready for it. The evening stretched ahead of them. She felt as if she had been shipwrecked on a heaving ocean, and there were still miles of grey sea to cross before she reached shore.

'It's all right, Christie,' came Lucas's taunting voice. 'You can look around now. I'm decent.'

She slowly turned her head, her blue eyes wide with anxiety.

He was wearing a white towelling robe which emphasised the pale gold of his skin. It contrasted strongly with the dark shadow of his unshaven chin. His arms were folded challengingly across his chest.

She took a deep breath and ran her tongue over her lips. When she stood up, she was horrified to discover that her knees were trembling. Boldly she took a couple of steps towards him 'Did...did you say something about sharing your bath?' she asked.

Lucas tilted his head to one side and surveyed her steadily. 'I did,' he said, his voice a low growl, 'but I didn't expect you to take me up on it.'

She gave a light laugh, which sounded silly and fraudulent, even to her own ears. 'Didn't you?' she continued desperately, taking a couple of steps closer to him. 'It sounds like a nice idea, don't you think?'

'No,' he replied and then turned on his heel and went through into the bathroom swiftly, banging the door firmly behind him.

Christie looked at the door in horror. Oh, lord. She'd done it again. She'd gone and given the impression that she was a worldly little seductress. All the back-pedalling in the world clearly couldn't erase the distasteful image she'd created of her London life. He didn't want her any more. And she couldn't possibly tell him the truth. If he knew that she'd only ever made love twice in her life he would know the whole story. He would start to feel trapped. The evening was still ahead of her. But dry land was no longer in sight.

When Lucas emerged from the bathroom, his wet hair brushed severely back from his brow, his skin damp and his chin freshly shaven, Christie was huddled under the bedclothes.

'What on earth are you doing there?' he muttered.

She peeped over the edge of the sheet. 'I've got a dreadful headache. I thought I'd have an early night.'

His bare feet separated so that he stood, feet apart, his toes curling into the thick blue carpet, his hands coming to rest contemptuously on his hips. 'But you haven't,' he said with unquestioning certainty.

'I have!'

'Aren't you hungry? Mrs Grey is preparing something quite special.'

She was hungry only for him. She closed her eyes briefly and suppressed a sigh. 'No. I'm not hungry.'

'Christie, I never imagined you'd be like this. You were always a gutsy little thing. What's happened to you?'

'Nothing.'

'Yes, it has. You've been like a cat on hot bricks since we got to the house.'

She put her hands over her face. 'I'll be all right once tomorrow is over,' she said wearily. 'I just can't face this evening.'

He came across to the bed and bent to catch hold of her wrist. And then he pulled. She slithered into a sitting position.

'Good grief!' he muttered, frowning and trying not to laugh at the same time. 'Those pyjamas! Christie!'

She snatched her wrist away from him and hurriedly folded her arms to disguise the swell of her throbbing breasts. She glanced down at her pink pyjamas, sprigged with little flowers. 'Oh, I know everything there is to know about keeping warm in bed. Remember, Lucas?' she muttered bitterly, and then lay down again.

He sighed. 'Have it your own way,' he returned breezily.

She stuck her head under the bedclothes and listened to the sounds of him getting dressed. She kept her head under the clothes until he had gone out of the room, and then came up for air.

A little later there was a tap at the door, and Lucas came in with a tray. 'Supper in bed,' he murmured, setting the tray on the table beside her. 'You're getting lazy, Christie,' he added with an air of decided satisfaction.

'Thank you, Lucas,' she replied stiffly. 'I'll try to eat something later.' Then she scowled, her expression making it plain that she didn't want him to stay. He tilted his head wryly and then left.

She sighed heavily, turning to the beautiful brass Benares-ware tray, polished until it shone like gold, and set with a light supper of prawns on a bed of salad, little triangles of bread and butter and a bowl of fruit *compote* with cream. Slowly she forced herself to eat the tempting little meal, but her appetite had quite gone. Later he would come to bed and she would have to try again to make him want her. When she had finished eating she got out of bed and took off her pyjamas. Then she slipped naked between the sheets and lay back to wait for him.

* * *

The curtains opened with an exuberant swoosh. Christie's eyes unglued themself. On the far side of the room stood Lucas, his back to her. He was completely naked. She blinked a few times. The sight of the hollow small of his back and the curve of his buttocks had instantly sent her pulses racing. She pulled the clothes over her head and groaned. It was morning already, and she'd slept right through the night. Which meant that today was their wedding-day, and still they hadn't anticipated the night to come. Oh, lord... How could she have been such a fool as to fall asleep?

'What's the matter, Christie?' came Lucas's voice. 'Did that tomato juice give you a hangover?'

Her head emerged from beneath the covers. 'No,' she said shortly. And then she winced as she saw him coming towards her, his powerful body outrageously tempting to her over-heated senses.

He pulled back the covers. 'Rise and shine,' he growled. 'We've got a busy day ahead.'

Now they were facing each other, both entirely naked. She looked up at Lucas. *Now*, a voice within her urged, as if daring her to fling herself over the edge of a precipice. He was leaning towards her a little, his eyes raking slowly over her.

'Why don't you come back to bed for five minutes, Lucas?' she whispered.

She saw his sinews tighten. His fists clenched so that his forearms hardened, and his thighs followed suit. He was becoming aroused before her eyes. She stared at him, her nipples hardening under the onslaught of his devouring gaze.

And then abruptly he straightened up and turned his back on her. 'Come on,' he said brusquely, his voice strained. 'Get up. We've got a lot to do.' And with a few swift steps he reached out and picked up his robe and put it on, belting it firmly. 'Your clothes are in the wardrobe.'

Christie tugged a sheet around her to cover the blush which was spreading over the entire expanse of her skin, enhancing rather than obliterating the flood of desire which had consumed her from the moment she opened her eyes and saw him. He, too, had been aroused at the sight of her—and yet still he didn't want her. Her heart seemed to tighten with anguish, like a closed fist. What was she to do?

As it happened she didn't have much choice about anything she did for the rest of the day. She bathed and washed her hair, took breakfast, again alone and from a tray, and then applied her make-up from the meagre collection in the toilet bag which Lucas had packed for her. When she opened the wardrobe she was confronted by a vast, empty space, interrupted only by a couple of her sweatshirts and clean jeans, and a single dress. It was the very dress she had worn to the party, five years ago: the dress she had chosen to attract Lucas's notice; the dress that had been the start of it all. Beneath it, on a shoe rack, were the high shoes with the little bows.

Her heart started to thud ominously when she saw the dress. She had three dresses—the other two were Indian cotton sunfrocks. There had been neither the occasion nor the money for Christie to buy herself another smart dress since that fateful summer. But *this* dress...to wear for her marriage to Lucas! She could understand why he had been forced to select it from her own wardrobe— and the shoes too. They were the only garments she possessed which were remotely suitable. She didn't for one moment imagine that *he* had remembered, or had had any particular motive in packing them. She looked wildly around the room for the print skirt and pink T-shirt, but they had gone.

Nervously she stepped into the dress, doing up the little buttons with trembling fingers. She opened a pair of tights and wriggled into them and then put her feet into the shoes. Then, feeing utterly unbridal, she went downstairs.

Lucas was waiting for her, looking immaculate in a dark lounge suit and crisp white shirt. He looked every inch the bridegroom. She felt painfully inadequate beside him.

And then Sarah came running up to greet her, wearing a blue bridesmaid's dress which perfectly matched her eyes, and blue, round-toed shoes. 'Mummy!' she exclaimed, with a happy smile. 'You look beautiful!'

'Thank you, darling,' said Christie, crouching down to bury her face in the child's hair so that Lucas wouldn't see her lower lip quivering and her eyes fill with tears. He'd arranged all this for Sarah, and yet had bought nothing at all for her. 'So do you,' she added kindly, bringing her emotions swiftly under control

'I hope the wedding doesn't take too long,' continued the little girl blithely. 'I have important things to do.'

'Have you?' Christie enquired weakly.

'Oh, yes. I've got somebody coming to fit me for my riding clothes, and Janine and me've got to arrange the special picnic in the stables. It's a lot of work.'

Christie stood up. 'You'll be very busy, then,' she said encouragingly.

And then Lucas helped her into her coat and lightly touched her elbow and led the way out to the Range Rover. He took her coat from her when they had pulled up outside the church and took her in on his arm, letting Sarah hold his other hand. Percy was waiting for them, beaming ecstatically. Marjorie Percival and old Mrs Percival, who lived with them, were sitting discreetly in a pew, ready to witness the event. Christie took a deep, tremulous breath. She felt faint, and had to force herself to breathe evenly and steadily. She had dreamed of this moment since she was a little girl. Now that it had come she was frightened to death.

When they came out of the church she was feeling strangely calm. All her fears had melted away as the old words of the service had been chanted for them. The very familiarity of the service seemed to draw her into a wider universe than the one she had previously inhabited. So many millions of women had trodden this path, all with their own stories to tell. She was just one among them. She had looked up at Lucas's face, and in the honest atmosphere of the Norman building she had let her love for him burn like a flame.

Out in the dank autumn air she made her way quietly back to the Range Rover and prepared to climb in. But Lucas simply grabbed her coat from the seat and said, 'Come on. We've got to go to the field behind the vicarage now.'

'Whatever for?' she asked, confused, thinking of ponies and picnics and apples.

'You'll see. Look, there's Janine. She'll take Sarah back to the house.'

What she saw when they got to the field was a helicopter, able to thwart any last traces of floodwater and take them straight to London, where a limousine awaited them. By half-past ten on the morning of her wedding Christie was in an exclusive London store, being greeted by an elegant fashion consultant.

'I'll meet you back at this entrance in a couple of hours...' said Lucas, with a lop-sided smile. 'I've got a little business to attend to.'

And with that he had gone, leaving her in the manicured hands of the consultant, with instructions to buy up the shop and have all her purchases packed into a set of matching luggage of her choice. Christie didn't allow herself to feel hurt. He was a busy man. He wouldn't want to hang around for hours while she was kitted out. She needed new clothes. She was his wife now. It was all perfectly straightforward.

When it was time to call a halt and Christie was positively exhausted from trying on the armfuls of clothes that were brought to her, she picked out a fine wool dirndl skirt and a huge matching overblouse with a bold pattern of purple and olive flowers and got dressed, slipping her feet into a pair of low-heeled shoes in soft purple leather. Then she allowed herself to be escorted back through the acreage of sales floors to meet up with Lucas again.

Lunch in an exclusive restaurant was followed by a flight in a private jet. By four in the afternoon Christie was being ushered through the portals of an expensive Paris hotel. At seven minutes past four Lucas put the key in the lock of their suite, and then scooped Christie up in his arms.

'I thought you didn't want to carry me over the threshold like a virgin bride,' she said worriedly.

He narrowed his eyes. 'I've changed my mind,' he said laconically, sweeping through the sitting-room to the bedroom beyond and laying her on a mound of satin-covered pillows.

'What now?' she asked shakily, fixing her blue eyes on his mouth.

The unforgiving line of his lips curled into a slow smile. 'What do you think?' he asked softly.

'You said you didn't want to... well, that is——'

'I know,' he interrupted, his dark eyebrows lifting wryly. 'But I've changed my mind about that as well. I'm afraid, Christie, that *you* no longer call the tune.'

Her heart gave a little lurch. She was unbelievably relieved. She wanted him so badly, and yet, having begun the whole saga by inviting him to take her, she had found it unbearably difficult to repeat the act of seduction—especially after he had twice rejected her. No doubt he also had come to the conclusion that it would be better to dress the whole business up in its traditional bridal garb. This was, after all, the honeymoon suite. The room was banked with flowers. Champagne and caviare stood on a gilt trolley in front of the window. The bed was vast, covered in a waste of white silk satin. And Lucas was sitting beside her, his breath coming roughly, and he was taking off her purple leather shoes.

He undressed them both completely before he so much as kissed her. His dry fingertips nudged at her flesh as he stripped away her new lacy underwear. They pressed against the fine skin of her thighs as he unfastened her silk stockings from their suspenders, and caressed the length of each of her legs in turn as he rolled the flimsy stockings back and discarded them on the floor. Christie sighed softly with pleasure, relishing the sense of engorgement that permeated her whole body. She needed him as a starving person needed food, and she couldn't help but be excited by the knowledge made manifest, as he discarded his own clothes, that he needed her too. His head and his heart might not want this marriage, but his flesh did. It made them quits. Her shyness fled, and by the time he was ready to come to lie beside her on the bed she was already offering her mouth, her lips slightly parted, to be kissed.

CHAPTER NINE

BEING kissed by Lucas was a kind of heaven. The moment his mouth touched hers she forgot everything. There was no future; no past; no right; no wrong. There was only the dry sensation of his lips brushing side to side over her own. He seemed to take an age before he increased the pressure and let his tongue explore her parted lips, and then quite abruptly, with a sudden abandonment of control, he plundered her mouth, so that they clung together, tongue meeting tongue, tasting each other's arousal in the deep urgency of the kiss.

His mouth travelled across the dips and hollows of her throat, coming to rest on one breast. As it met the swell he paused as if frozen, his breath flowing warm across her skin, caressing her excited nipple, tantalising her senses. She remained motionless, savouring the mounting pleasure of anticipation, until at long last his mouth began to move again, more harshly, dragging across her breast until it captured the nipple between his firm lips. The rush of desire which accompanied the sensation of her nipple being drawn deep into his mouth had her arching against him, so that she felt the powerful bulk of his muscular body crushed against her own. His thigh parted hers, strong, demanding, stirring hard against the sharp punches of pleasure which assailed her from deep inside.

Christie began to moan breathlessly. Her need was becoming overpowering. She wanted to feel the dark maleness of him cleaving her flesh, making them one, carrying her inflamed senses out of the confines of her body to explode into a wider universe. Rippling; pulsing; satisfying. They were urging each other with their flesh, digging and nipping and tasting. She wanted him... She wanted him oh, so badly... But there was something... something...

She dragged her mouth away from the curve of his shoulder. 'Lucas,' she breathed. 'I'm not... you know... on the Pill or anything.' Her voice was shuddering with desire.

'It's OK,' he groaned dismissively, as if her words had no place in the world they inhabited.

'Aren't you... I mean, haven't you got anything...?'

'I'm not going to stop,' he said, his voice thick with desire. 'I can't...'

Then Lucas froze. He closed his eyes and his face contorted and he bit down on his lower lip. And then he thrust hard against her. Her flesh opened to him, moist, suffused with desire, welcoming. The sensation of him moving within her was overpowering. There had been thoughts in her mind, words on her tongue, but they were spilling away as her blood screamed out its urgent response to their union. Rhythmically, smoothly, every movement dictated by an atavistic instinct, she moved beyond thought into the realm of pure sensation. Her lips sought his skin and her teeth bit into his flesh as each thrust sent a sharp resonance quivering through her. She was having to drag in each breath, gasping as her excitement clambered frantically upwards, until suddenly she took that one last quivering breath which tipped her headily into the final response. From his flesh came an answering cry, and motionless, not breathing, they gripped each other in a still frenzy of thundering pleasure.

When the inner turbulence ended her mind seemed to crack wide open. She began to breathe again, her body spent and boneless beneath his, her eyes seeing only the hot red of her blood as it moved again in her veins, her ears hearing only the thudding of her heart, her skin wet and hot and satiated. Lucas. He had married her. He had chosen to make love with her. He had not been able to help himself, even when he knew the risk. She was, briefly, sublimely happy.

At last he rolled off her and, face down on the sheets sank into oblivion. She too could not hold sleep at bay. They were claimed, like powerless infants, by its hazy force. She didn't know how long they slept, but when she awoke the light had faded in the room to a crepuscular grey and Lucas was nuzzling at her breasts with an eager tongue. She opened her eyes a crack and caught the dark glitter of his eyes, black and shining in the colourless room. Her shoulders came back and her spine arched so that she offered him the plenty of her soft flesh in a gesture as instinctive as it was slight. She clasped his head between her hands, resting her fingers on his cheeks, aroused by the male prickle of his skin against her palms. She buried her face in the thick, straight, clean hair of his head, and smelt sweat and skin behind the hard, artificial tang of shampoo and soap. Her tongue darted out and tasted his brow, warm and salt and male, stretched cleanly over the hard bone, while he sucked rhythmically on the bursting buds of her breasts. Here, in bed, they were surely married in every sense.

In the middle of the evening he stretched lazily, then sat up and got out of bed. He put on his robe, and fetched her new silky gown and held it out for her. 'Come on,' he said with an impatient sigh. 'Hurry up.'

'What are we doing?' she asked.

He led her out on to the balcony. The lights of Paris blazed before them. 'There you are,' he said brusquely. 'You can come back in now.'

'I don't understand.' She frowned, as they went back into the room.

Lucas gave one of his bitingly acute smiles. 'We've got to go back tomorrow. If people ask what you thought of Paris, won't you find it embarrassing if you have to admit that you didn't actually see it? Well, now you've seen it.'

Christie let out an exclamation of laughter. 'I thought you didn't care what people thought,' she said, suddenly recognising the man and loving him all the more.

'And I thought *you* did,' he responded, throwing off his robe and joining her in the bed. 'You do, don't you, Christie? You keep telling me that you do, so it's no good denying it.' He was taunting her now, in such a familiar way that she wanted to shout with pleasure.

'But you can't believe anything I say, surely?' she mocked back.

And then Lucas froze. He rolled on to one side and propped his head in his hand. 'Well,' he said slowly, 'let's not go into that too deeply now,' and he reached out a hand to stroke her.

She edged away. 'Lucas?' she said pleadingly.

He withdrew his hand and sighed heavily. 'I expect your family will be delighted to know that you're married at last,' he uttered, and a sour smile tightened his mouth.

Christie's stomach clenched against the hurt. That momentary understanding had been an illusion. 'I expect they'll be extremely pleased for me,' she agreed vacantly.

Lucas stretched. He took in a deep breath which expanded his ribcage and made a deep hollow of his abdomen. All the hairs on his chest stood up. 'I'm damned sure they will be. But whether they are or aren't is no concern of mine.'

'Lucas?' whispered Christie. 'I know I lied to you, but——'

'Oh, shut up, Christie. I've told you before that the past is a closed book.'

She lay in silence, her eyes aching.

Lucas sat up and swung his legs over the side of the bed. 'Champagne, Christie?' he asked cynically.

Christie swallowed hard on her disappointment. 'Do we have anything to celebrate?' she asked nervously.

'Oh, yes,' he said, getting up and walking over to the trolley. 'We can celebrate the fact that you're a respectable married woman at last. And we can also drink to the fact that you're going to stay that way for the rest of your life.'

She pulled her wrap a little tighter around herself. It must be at least seventy-five degrees in this room, but she felt chilled none the less. In Lucas's eyes she was a silly little stablemaid who'd made a mess of her life. Now she was well set up as the wife of Lucas Merrick. Hadn't she done well for herself?

'I don't want this marriage to be a trap, Lucas,' she said with a sudden vehemence. 'You married me for Sarah's sake. Well, that's fair enough. It's why I married you, too. But that doesn't mean that it has to be a cage. I shan't make demands on you, you know...'

He turned and looked at her so coldly that she almost cried out aloud. Then, the champagne dangling from one hand, he crossed the room and caught hold of her chin with the other hand. 'Is this some kind of reciprocal arrangement you're trying to set up here, Christie? Because, if so, let me tell you that I won't wear it. I certainly plan to make demands on you now that you're my wife. I shall expect a very great deal from you, Christabel Merrick. A very great deal indeed...'

'You've got it wrong!' she protested. 'I didn't mean that. I simply meant that...that...' She opened her hands helplessly and sighed.

Lucas let go of her chin and turned away.

'Lucas,' she continued insistently, 'I didn't marry you for respectability or anything like that. I consider I had everything I needed in life before we even agreed to marry. You don't seem to understand that I'm good at my job, and it's very secure at present. Steven would love me to do more for him, and——'

'I'll bet he damned well would,' bit out Lucas scathingly. 'And I'm so reassured to know that you already had *everything* you wanted in life. Aren't you lucky? Now you have even more!'

Christie buried her face in her hands. 'I've already told you that there's never been anything like that between Steven and me,' she sighed shakily.

Lucas's eyes glanced to one side, as if he could no longer bear to look at her. 'So you did, Christie,' he said wearily. 'Now let's not talk about it any more, huh?'

So they didn't. And they didn't drink the champagne. Nor did they use the jacuzzi in the sumptuous bathroom. Instead they each took a quick shower and returned to the chill of the warm room. Lucas ordered a meal from Room Service. Then he switched on the television. It was in French, and Christie couldn't follow it. She sauntered over to the bureau near the window and found headed stationary and a pen with the hotel's name on it. She took paper and pen to bed and drew some flow charts for the program she was working on. But without her papers to refer to, it was a waste of time.

* * *

The picnic with the horses took place just as soon as they arrived back. Lucas was breezy, Sarah excited, Christie nonplussed. She sat on a bale of hay and watched father and daughter dishing out apples to the big animals on the flat of their hands. She sauntered over to join them, and fondled the velvety muzzle of a bay mare with her fingertips.

'I thought you didn't like horses any more,' said Lucas frostily.

'Whatever gave you that idea?'

'Oh, just something you said to that effect.'

'When did I say that? I couldn't have. I've always loved horses.'

'Early one morning in May, Christie.'

'Oh. Yes. I remember now. But I didn't mean it.'

'Why did you say it, then?'

'Because...' She looked at him frantically. 'Because I didn't want you to think that I...' She tailed off miserably. Because I didn't want you to think that I must be in love with you... She took a deep breath. 'Because I was annoyed with you.'

The corners of his mouth turned down. 'So do I have to weigh the truth of everything you say according to your mood?'

Christie blew out a sigh. 'Does it really matter?' she sighed wearily, meeting his eye.

'Oh, yes, Christie,' he muttered in a voice both low and infinitely dangerous. 'It matters a great deal.'

'Lucas, I know that there's been... well...misunderstandings between us, and we both know that I wasn't truthful with you about certain things, but can't you stop carping about it? Not for my sake, Lucas. I...I guess I deserve it all. But for Sarah's.'

Lucas gave her an implacable look. 'I wouldn't say anything untoward if we had Sarah's attention. Surely you realise that by now?'

'Yes. You're very loving with her. I know that you wouldn't do anything in the world to hurt her.'

'Then you really want me to stop reminding you of your past...inadequacies...for your own sake. Not hers.'

Christie shook her head. 'No, Lucas. For *her* sake. Honestly. I'm afraid that I'll become too wretched if I have to face disbelief from you at every turn. Sarah isn't used to me that way. No matter how hard I try to put a good face on it I'm afraid she'll come to sense the change in me. I'm *not* asking you for my own sake. It is for hers.'

There was a long silence. 'How round your eyes have grown, Christie,' he said slowly. 'Like saucers.'

She sensed his disdain and looked away. She had lied to him about so many things. But only because she loved him so. Only because she didn't want to spoil his life. And yet that was exactly what she was doing without even trying. In the dark of night they had a perfect marriage. In the cold of day it was a painful parody.

She wandered over towards Sarah. The child was her protector. He wouldn't say anything hurtful now. She crouched down beside the child and laid her cheek against her daughter's fine skin. 'Are you happy, darling?' she asked softly.

Sarah turned her serious blue eyes on her mother's. 'I'm so happy,' she said steadily, 'that I feel as if I've swallowed one of these apples.' She tapped her chest just beneath her breastbone. 'There's a happy apple there. I can feel it.'

Tears washed over the surface of Christie's eyes and then soaked away. Sarah. This was all for her. It had been the right thing to do, after all, and she would work hard at pleasing Lucas and learn to guard her tongue and everything would be fine. If only she'd remembered that she'd claimed back in May that she no longer liked horses he wouldn't have said any of those painful things. It was her own stupid fault as usual. If she just thought a little harder before she opened her mouth everything would be just fine.

It was moderately fine that evening, as it happened. She spoke very carefully, judging her words and keeping her tone of voice light, and Lucas responded with not a single scathing comment. The fire burned brightly in the hearth and Christie grew quite optimistic. And it was certainly fine in bed that night.

In the morning Lucas rose early to see to the horses, and Christie breakfasted alone from the Benares-ware tray.

She dressed carefully in conker-brown cord trousers, teamed with a matching sweater and a cream angora cardigan, and applied some of her new make-up to her anxious face. Yes. She looked like the right sort of wife for Lucas Merrick today. Unless you happened to know that Lucas hadn't wanted any sort of wife in the first place.

Janine had already taken Sarah to playgroup when she came downstairs. She went and sat in the big, galleried room and found a crossword in an old colour supplement to occupy her. But Mrs Grey and the daily help came in with polish and vacuum cleaner and a large bowl of fresh flowers. Christie fled back upstairs and rang her father and her aunts. They were, indeed, delighted, and asked not one awkward question, but simply poured out their heartfelt congratulations and good wishes. She couldn't help wondering as she put down the phone just exactly what the miserable old pair of Merricks would make of their only son's marriage.

In the end she trailed back to the cottage to get on with some work. Already it seemed uninhabited, even though Sarah's colouring-book was still open on the table and the ashes were barely cold in the grate. She went upstairs and set to work on her last program. When this was finished she would no longer be the independent young woman who had coped so admirably with single parenthood at such a tender age. She would be Christabel Merrick, wife of the local landowner and breeder of bloodstock. She smiled bitterly. Lucas had once said that he shopped around for a suitable stallion for his mares. He could trace his own bloodline back through generations. Nobody who saw him could doubt that he was a thoroughbred. Would he ever, given a free choice, have brought her into his stable?

Later she collected Sarah from playgroup, and drove her back to Home Farm. Lucas was waiting for them, dressed comfortably in cords and an Aran sweater, his hands on his hips.

'Did you have a good morning?' he asked, smiling.

'Yes...' said Christie with a smile, but her voice tailed away as she realised that his question had been directed at the little girl.

'Oh, it was lovely. We did painting today, and I did a picture just for you, Daddy. I haven't even shown it to Mummy yet. She wanted to look but I wouldn't let her. I said it was yours.'

Lucas crouched down and took the rolled-up painting from the child. 'That was very kind of you, Sarah,' he said softly. 'And I'm honoured. I really am. But why don't Mummy and I unroll it and look at it together?

Your mother's very special too, and it would be nice if we could think the painting was for both of us.'

Christie smiled politely as Lucas brought the painting across for her to share. Nothing Sarah could do or say could hurt her—she understood and loved her child far too much for that. And anyway, she was genuinely pleased that father and daughter had forged such a strong bond so swiftly. And yet she *was* hurt. She was hurt because all this tender concern of Lucas's was centred on his child. He was encouraging Sarah to include her mother in the viewing of the masterpiece in order to help the little girl learn good manners.

'And where did you get to this morning, Christie?' he asked at last.

'I went back to the cottage to work.'

He frowned at her. 'I see,' he said. 'How long is it going to take you to finish this job?'

'I'm not sure. About a week, I think. It depends on how many hours I can put in.'

Lucas's frown deepened and hardened. 'I'll get someone to bring your computer up here. You can finish it more quickly then.'

'But I... Very well. If that's what you want.'

'Shouldn't I?'

'Oh...yes. Of course you should. It's an excellent idea, Lucas. I'll be very grateful to have the computer brought here.'

He sighed. 'Have you rung the agency and told them you won't be taking on any more work?'

'Not yet. You see, I... I'll do it soon.'

His lips made a straight line. 'Do it this afternoon.'

'Yes, Lucas.'

Guarding her tongue wasn't that difficult after all. It was very unpleasant, though. It was...stifling. It felt as though she had a huge piece of indiarubber in her hand and had just erased her own mouth. Presumably it would be much easier once she had managed to erase her own heart as well.

They played chess that evening and she drank white wine while he had Scotch. Mrs Grey provided a wonderful meal. Christie took a leisurely bath before bed. Lucas joined her in the bathroom. He came in, his face as hard and set as it had been all evening, though his tone, when he had spoken, had been easier.

Christie looked down at the water bathing her limbs. She was painfully aware of her nakedness. She felt ashamed: as if she were seducing him into something he didn't really want all over again. And then Lucas tilted his chin and smiled a dry smile and said, 'Worried about the cost of leaving the boiler running all evening, Christie?'

'No. Not so long as I don't have to earn the money to pay the bills.'

'So being married to me does have its compensations after all?'

She flashed him a brief look, but said nothing. It was all very well, guarding her tongue. But finding the correct bland response was another matter.

He smiled again and his eyes glittered shamelessly. 'Let's see if I can't persuade you of a few more compensations to our wedded state, huh?'

And then he came and knelt beside her and trailed one finger across her shoulder and down her breast until he cupped its heavy fullness in his palm, and then he kissed her neck. She closed her eyes. When they made love there was no need to search for the right responses. They came unbidden, as if they were, in every respect, a perfectly matched pair.

Her computer arrived the next morning, and was set up in a corner of Lucas's study. It seemed odd to see its familiar screen in this new location. But right and proper, she reminded herself dutifully. The cottage was no longer her home. And the sooner she finished this work and got on with the business of becoming a good wife to Lucas, the better. If it would please Lucas for her to sever this last tie, then she had better hurry up and do it.

And when Sarah brought an eggbox home from playgroup that day—a perfectly ordinary eggbox with simply one tiny scrap of blue tissue paper glued messily to its lid—and refused to show it to either of her parents without the other being present—because it was a dragon and too frightening to be viewed alone—and Lucas put his arm around his wife's shoulder in the most comradely and comforting of ways while they inspected the fearsome box, Christie began to feel that it was all coming together at last. It would all work out, if only she could master her tongue.

'Our daughter's a creative genius, isn't she, Christie? A minimalist sculptor in the making... Shall we ring the Royal Academy?'

She rubbed her hand unconsciously across her mouth before she replied. 'She's certainly very clever, Lucas,' she murmured meekly.

She worked all afternoon. And part of the evening. She wanted to complete the job for Lucas's sake, and she had to admit it was the perfect excuse for keeping out of Lucas's way during the day. She didn't actually want to keep out of his way at night. He, clearly, felt pretty much the same.

The next day was a Saturday. Lucas took her and Sarah into Gloucester to buy clothes for the little girl.

When Sarah was around Lucas mellowed. His dry humour surfaced, and he was easy, relaxing company. He was also unbelievably decisive. While Christie tentatively brushed her hand along a rack of dresses in the children's boutique, Lucas was piling garments on to the counter and firing questions at the assistant. 'So where do you think we'll be able to get good waterproofs in her size? Uh huh... And footwear...? And some smart sweaters; I don't like those fluorescent ones, which seem to be all you have...'

Christie enjoyed the day. Sarah enjoyed the white, pointy, unsuitable shoes. And they didn't stop at shopping for Sarah, either. Lucas led the way to a few adult boutiques and ordered her to pick out some stuff for herself.

'I haven't worn a quarter of the clothes we bought in London,' she complained.

Lucas smiled, the lines on his face breaking into unfamiliar curves, his auburn eyes shining. 'Oh, dear. You always were obsessed by mathematics,' he sighed, one eyebrow crooking itself humorously. 'So how many garments will you need to buy not to have worn seven-eighths of them? Or, more complexly, not to have worn point one seven of them? Now come on, Christie... get that old brain of yours into gear...'

She flapped her hands. 'I've probably already worn point one seven of them,' she muttered, her quick brain grasping the joke immediately. 'But that's not the point,' she added helplessly.

'Isn't it? Oh. So what is the point?'

'Well, it just seems a bit... wasteful.'

He shook his head. 'Wasteful? But I'm not asking you to throw the others away unworn.'

'I know, but——'

'But I tell you what. Wear four or five layers of clothes at a time for a few days. Then you'll soon have worn all of them and you won't feel so bad about it. Of course,' he added, running his eyes over her figure, 'it will spoil the view for me for a few days, but I guess I can bear the sacrifice as long as you compromise by wearing absolutely nothing in bed.'

Christie blushed furiously, glancing around to check that nobody was listening. Nobody was. She looked tentatively back at him. Oh, if only it could always be like this...

But it didn't stay like that for long. Lucas appeared that evening looking tired and bad-tempered. He got himself a drink, slumped in his chair by the fire, and said, 'We've been invited to the Manor for Sunday lunch tomorrow.'

Christie gulped. 'Your parents know that we're—er...?' She tailed off weakly.

'The word's "married", Christie. It has more than four letters. I won't make you wash your mouth out with soap if you speak it aloud. And the answer is yes. They do know we're married.'

'What do they think?'

He shrugged carelessly. 'Who cares?' he said, and then raised his newspaper and began to read.

Christie was frightened to death when they set off, all dressed up, at twelve-thirty the following day. Matters weren't helped when Lucas's faded mother held out a droopy hand to be shaken and said, 'Fancy Lucas marrying a village girl. He did surprise us. But I do hope you'll be happy all the same...'

His corpulent father stared at Christie and said nothing. Then he turned to Lucas and muttered quite audibly from the side of his mouth, 'Pretty little filly.

Bit of schooling and you'll have a champion on your hands.'

Lucas gave his father a withering look. Then he turned to his mother and said, 'Thank you for your good wishes, Mother. I can assure you that Christie and I are already happier than you could possibly imagine.'

Christie bit her lip. She wanted to laugh. Given his parents' notoriously miserable dispositions, it was hardly a positive comment on the state of their own new marriage! But she felt unaccountably safe all of a sudden. Lucas might be dismayed by his wife, but he'd never let his parents suspect that their union was anything less than perfect.

Indeed he didn't. He proudly introduced his daughter to her lugubrious grandparents and then carried off the whole of the remainder of the occasion with such soaring panache that both Christie and Sarah were made to feel the most cherished possessions a man could have.

Once Christie had finished her work she had to struggle to find a new pattern for her life. She had Sarah with her in the afternoons and at weekends, but now she had to share her daughter with Lucas and Janine in a way that she'd never had to share her before. Sarah was a confident, outgoing child. She thrived on the extra attention she received, and Christie was pleased for her. But it didn't help fill the lonely hours. Lucas worked incredibly hard, and was often off the estate. When he went away she would ride. She had never been terribly good on horseback, despite her enthusiasm, but she enjoyed it all the same.

One morning Lucas surprised her by bringing her breakfast in himself. He set down the gleaming tray and then sat on the edge of the bed and watched her sip her cup of tea.

'We've been married for well over a month now,' he said shortly at last.

'Yes.'

'You haven't had a period yet.'

Christie set down her cup. 'No...' she agreed, feeling alarmed.

'Are you usually regular?'

She looked at him, panic-stricken. 'Usually, but it's quite possible to miss a couple when——'

'When was it due?'

'About twelve days ago, but, the thing is, when something fairly major happens in life it quite often——'

'You're pregnant, then,' announced Lucas, standing up and rubbing his palms down over his jodhpurs with an air of distinct satisfaction. 'Good.'

'If I am, then——'

'You are.'

She nodded slowly. She had sensed, once or twice, a faint prickling in her breasts. She was almost sure herself... 'Why are you so pleased?' she blurted out frantically.

But Lucas just said sharply, 'You don't want Sarah to be an only child, do you?'

'No. But I still don't understand why you're so pleased.'

Lucas said nothing in reply. He just gave her a caustic smile and then left the room with a decidedly jaunty air.

CHAPTER TEN

THE pregnancy was confirmed a week later by the local GP. Lucas was nicer to her, on the whole, but she got the distinct impression that it was a temporary state, induced by her condition. She had been alarmed when she had discovered that she was carrying Sarah. Alarmed and excited and pleased. The circumstances hadn't been right, but she had rejoiced for the new life she carried within her—and for the fact that the new life was a part of Lucas. She felt exactly the same this time around.

The only difference was the fact that this time Lucas was clearly so pleased. And it wasn't just on Sarah's account, either. He gave off the air of a man who was, in one respect at least, supremely satisfied with life. There could be no doubt that Lucas wanted this baby.

He found her one afternoon, grooming Soloman.

'What the hell are you doing that for?' he said brusquely.

'I like doing it.'

'You should rest.'

She dithered, unsure what to say. Lots of men were over-protective when their wives were pregnant—or so she'd heard. But she didn't feel like an invalid, and was sure there was no reason why she shouldn't do most things in moderation. Cagily she said, 'But Lucas, really——'

He sighed irritably. 'Go and sit down inside. I'm going to ring your aunt and get her to come and stay to make sure you rest.'

He was treating her like the incompetent child he had always imagined her to be. 'I don't need to rest,' she complained, but Lucas wasn't listening.

A car brought Aunt Sassy all the way from London. She was thrilled to be back in the village, and especially thrilled to be with Christie and Sarah again. Christie hadn't wanted her aunt to come. She was having enough trouble as it was, getting the hang of this marriage. Aunt Sassy was too sharp-eyed by far. But she couldn't help being pleased to see her, none the less.

'Another baby!' she said, throwing up her hands with delight as two of the stable lads struggled awkwardly to heave her out of the car and prop her on her walking frame. 'Best news I've had for weeks.'

She held court in the sitting-room, greeting Maudie and Mrs Brewer and Ellen and Tommy and all the others who flocked to greet their old friend.

Lucas and Sassy got on particularly well.

'How're you doing, you old devil?' Lucas said, smiling, his eyes sharpening with incipient mirth. When he sat down opposite Aunt Sassy he stretched out his legs and stuck his hands behind the back of his neck as if he was truly at ease.

'Old devil indeed!' returned Aunt Sassy, her eyes bright. 'Still, it takes one to know one. But don't go calling me that in front of other people. I've got my reputation to think of—unlike your good self. You've always gone out of your way to make people think the worst of you, Lucas Merrick. And I doubt you've ever been disappointed on that score.'

'Only where *you're* concerned,' returned Lucas sharply. 'But I don't flatter myself that it's to my credit that you choose to think well of me. It's simply that you enjoy swimming against the tide. It suits your self-image to like me. No more, no less.'

Christie's heart sank as she watched them sparring together. She felt an uncomfortable sense of recognition as she skirted the challenging atmosphere they created between them. Once, a very long time ago, when she was thirteen and fourteen and fifteen, she and Lucas had been like that together, as they played chess at the vicarage, or caught loose horses, or exchanged knowing looks when the miserable old pair appeared on the scene. Except that then she had not seen what she was able to see now. She had been too young to understand that Lucas positively relished the cut and thrust of such dangerous dialogue.

His caustic remarks were not intended to hurt. He used them to create a conspiracy of unspoken understanding. Once she understood that, she was elated at the idea that he had at one time included her in his intrigue. But her elation collapsed when she realised how many years had passed since he had played such verbal games with her. Lucas had decided a long time ago she was too juvenile to merit his attention.

Aunt Sassy settled in well, despite disapproving of being forced to watch television in what she termed a 'glorified barn'. She claimed she could still smell cows in there. Like Sarah and Lucas's parents, Sassy's company also proved to be protection against Lucas's tongue. He was always civilised and courteous to Christie in her aunt's presence. Christie should have been grateful, but in fact she felt uneasy. She would rather have her regular reminders of how Lucas really felt about her. She could grow complacent on this congeniality, and where would that get her?

When Canon Percival came to visit, Christie was the one to answer the door. 'My dear! Such excellent news... And your dear aunt with you, too. You must be truly joyful.'

Aunt Sassy's rubber-tipped sticks squeaked on the polished floor behind them.

'No, she's not, Percy,' announced Sassy. 'The poor scrap's as miserable as sin. Of course she won't tell me what it's all about. I'm only her blooming aunty. She'll tell you, though, won't you, Christie?'

'There's nothing to tell,' sighed Christie, glaring over her shoulder at her aunt. 'I'm very happy, Canon Percival. Honestly. I don't know why Aunt Sassy should think that.'

'Huh!' scoffed her aunt, eyeing the clergyman knowingly.

Christie made her excuses and fled. She changed into an old pair of jeans and a sweatshirt and anorak and went out to saddle the steady little mare she usually rode. It was December now. The trees were bare and the sky a wintry grey.

She cantered over the soft ground, her hands cold, her cheeks apple-red as the wind whipped colour into them. It was good out here on the horse. She was away from all the things which threatened to overwhelm her. Lucas. Mostly Lucas. Entirely Lucas, really. Only Sarah still could bring a smile of pure pleasure to her face.

She rode until she felt easier in herself, and was about to turn back when she heard Lucas's voice hailing her from a distance. She looked over her shoulder. He was holding the head of a big, dark horse, way off in the distance. She ducked her head, pretending not to hear him, and nudged the mare onwards. She really couldn't face a dose of Lucas right now. It wasn't long before she heard the thunder of hoofs behind her. Another cautious glance revealed Lucas, riding bareback, heading in her direction at a furious pace. She made for the woods behind the cottage. He couldn't ride among the branches. Perhaps he'd turn back when he saw where she'd gone.

When he found her she was sitting astride the old felled tree. It was damp and mossy now, and she could feel the chill penetrating her clothes.

'What the hell are you up to?' he blazed.

'I'm sorry, Lucas.' She sighed meekly. 'I should have come when you called.'

He marched towards her, his fist raised as if to strike her, anger scratched horribly all over his face. She flinched. It had been rude of her to ignore him, but she really couldn't understand why he should be so wild. He lowered his fist when he got close, and stood with his hands on his hips, glaring at her furiously.

'Bitch!' he snarled between clenched teeth.

Christie looked up at him in alarm. She was dreadfully shocked by what she read in his face. He *hated* her. Poor Lucas. No matter how hard she tried she was never going to make him happy. Tears of regret filled her eyes. She should never have forced him to acknowledge that Sarah was his child. She had known intuitively that it was the wrong thing to do, but she'd done it on impulse and now he was having to pay the price. He hadn't wanted to know.

'I'm sorry,' she murmured greyly.

'No, you're not!' he challenged bitterly. 'You keep acting like some kind of cowering, slavering dog when I'm around. But I'm not fooled for one minute, Christie. You're not sorry at all.'

She looked up at him. His face was almost unrecognisable.

'I *am* sorry, Lucas, believe it or not. More sorry than I can say.' Mortification stung her as she surveyed the evidence of his hatred written in his contorted features.

He looked around him. 'This is the clearing where you told me that Sarah wasn't my child,' he spat out cruelly.

She couldn't bring herself to reply.

'Lies...' he continued tautly, his breath fogging the air. His mouth was hard with disdain. 'All lies, Christie. Well, we're not staying here so that I can listen to any more of your wretched lies. You can start walking back home now. Slowly. Then you can have a warm shower and go to bed. I'll get the doctor to come and take a look at you.'

'The doctor? Lucas, that's ridiculous... Why on earth should I...?' She cut herself off. 'Very well, Lucas,' she sighed incomprehendingly. 'Whatever you say.'

His hand shot out and grasped her shoulder. He stared down at her with a ferocity which appalled her. 'Stop it!' he roared. 'Stop behaving that way! I can't stand it!'

'What way?' she muttered, trying to wriggle out of his painful grasp. She was frightened now. He was so angry... and all this stuff about the doctor. She really didn't understand...

'Yes, sir. No, sir. Three bags full, sir. Why are you doing it? Are you trying to make me pay for forcing this marriage on you? Is that why you keep imitating the way my mother behaves with my father? If so, then it's in the worst possible taste!'

'No!' she exclaimed indignantly. 'It never even occurred to me...' And then, appallingly, she wanted to laugh, because he was right. That was exactly the way his mother behaved with his father. She dared not laugh, though. She knew that it would enrage him even further. 'Look, Lucas... all I've been trying to do is to be agreeable. That's all.'

'And you think that it could possibly please me to have you simpering away like a rag doll stuffed full of milky rice pudding? Liar!'

'Believe it or not, that *is* all I want to do, Lucas.'

'That and lose the baby.'

'What?'

'That's why you went out riding today, isn't it?'

'No! Lucas, how could you say something like that?' She was genuinely horrified by the accusation. It told in every line of her face.

Lucas paused for a moment, then let go of her shoulder. 'I'm sorry I said that,' he said bitterly. 'But you frightened me badly when I saw you galloping like that.'

She glared at him unforgivingly. 'I'm fit and healthy and young, Lucas. It shouldn't hurt anything for me to ride a little.' She swallowed hard. 'It was a dreadful thing to say.'

He shrugged coldly. 'I've apologised. I guess I never quite got over your decision to have an abortion last time. I mean, I know you didn't go through with it, and you were only eighteen, so I could hardly blame you, but even so——'

'What are you talking about, Lucas?' she cried indignantly. 'I never threatened to have an abortion! The idea never even crossed my mind.'

Now it was Lucas's turn to look at her with palpable disbelief. 'You told me right here in this clearing. Or was that just another of your lies? Lies which were so trivial and unimportant that you couldn't even be bothered to remember them.'

'I...I didn't say it, Lucas,' she whispered.

He shrugged. 'No. You've forgotten. That's all. Actually, I couldn't imagine that you really meant it—even at the time. But you were in the business of selling me a pack of lies anyway, that day. What difference could one more make? But I haven't forgotten anything, Christie. I can remember every word you said...every little expression on your face... I can remember it all. But you probably don't even remember that we had that conversation right here in this spot, do you?'

Christie looked up at the wounded tree. It was young and strong. Even bare of leaves, it looked straight and true and healthy. The scar from the broken branch had resolved into a neat grey whorl. Trees, it seemed, healed easily. 'I remember,' she said softly. 'And I didn't say anything about an abortion.' She was suddenly assailed by a painful anger. 'How could I have when I was an accidental child myself? My mother had a weak heart... She'd been warned. Even so, she wanted me to be born. As I did with Sarah, from the very first minute. And as I do with this new baby too.' She laid her hands tenderly on her flat abdomen. She seemed to draw strength from the gesture. She had to speak out now to protect her unborn child. The baby couldn't hear or understand—but it was there with her, and she couldn't let the accusation lie.

She shook her thick golden-brown hair away from her bright blue eyes. 'I did lie to you, Lucas. I thought it was for the best. But I'm not lying about that. I don't know what it was I said that gave you the idea that I was contemplating...something like that. But you got it wrong. Badly wrong.'

He stared at her. 'You said that it was your body—your choice. I...' He sighed, frowning. 'It seemed very straightforward. I never even thought to question it. After we made love you insisted that you couldn't possibly be pregnant, you see. You were so young—so unknowing... I didn't see how you could possibly be so certain—unless you were just too immature to handle the idea and were... well, pushing the possibility out of your mind in some way. So when you said that you were going to choose not to have your life ruined, well, it seemed obvious what you intended. That's why I begged you to have it adopted. For goodness' sake, Christie, why else would I have asked you to do that if I hadn't thought you were contemplating something worse?'

She bit hard on her upper lip. 'Because you didn't like children, Lucas. I admit you've changed since you got to know Sarah, and I think you're a fine father, so I don't want to labour the point. But you hated them then.'

He shook his head. 'You're accusing *me* of lying now,' he said.

Christie looked across at Lucas with infinite love and infinite sadness. His head was tilted, as if to let his words catch the sun. But there was no sun, only a grey wintry light filtering between the bare branches of the trees. Spring was a long way off. And this conversation was destroying whatever shreds of good intent had held their brief marriage together so far.

'No,' she said softly at last. 'Not that. Or at least, I think you're sort of lying to yourself. It seems you have a habit of doing that. I *can* understand why you... you chose to misunderstand whatever it was I said that day, you see.'

'You think I lie to *myself*?'

'Yes.'

'For crying out loud, why should you think that?'

Because, she thought, because you are strong and fearless and determined. For you the world is black and white. You live your life according to such clear dictates that you do not see the muddled greys which cloud the truths of people's lives, and blur the edges.

'Does it really matter?' she said softly. 'The point is that, either way, you didn't think it appropriate that I should raise my child myself. No matter who the father was. What would you have said if I'd told you *then* that Sarah was yours?'

'I'd have asked you to marry me, of course.'

He sounded so certain. And oh, it was such a painful thing to hear. Was it true, or was he fooling himself again? He loved Sarah now. He wanted this new baby. Had he made the world afresh in this new image...? Turned black, miraculously, to white? She shook her head sadly. 'I don't believe you, Lucas,' she said shakily, and looked back at the wounded tree.

She didn't get a chance to study it in any great depth. Lucas's fingers grasped her chin and he turned her face to his. 'What the hell are you on about? I know you're determined to make me regret marrying you, but this is absurd. Of course I would have married you!'

Christie flung out an arm and knocked his hand away. She was roaring inside with a wild, despairing rage. How could they ever solve their problems if he kept forcing these truths out into the open...? A few more bitter accusations and she would be admitting that she had never known any man except him—that she had loved him for as long as she could remember. And then he would know why he hated her and he would feel trapped and resentful, and if they stayed together the children would suffer, and if they didn't... Well, if they didn't she could hardly imagine that she would survive. Lying beside Lucas every night, making love with him, had filled such an aching void in her life that she knew she could never bear the loss.

'Stop it, Lucas!' she cried. 'Stop saying these things! You didn't want marriage then... You didn't want children. You hated the very idea!'

'Christie, it's not true!'

She buried her face in her hands. 'It is true...' she muttered.

He caught hold of her arm. 'It's not good for you, getting so upset. And it's cold. You'd better come back home and calm down,' he said in a tight, strained voice.

'There's more you want to say, isn't there?' she bit out sourly.

He nodded slowly. 'Yes. But I shan't say it. It would do no good. Now come home and try to calm down.'

Obediently she began to follow him, his hand still grasping her wrist. They collected the horses and led them slowly back across the fields.

When they arrived back Canon Percival had gone and Sassy was busy crocheting. Lucas had his arm around Christie's shoulder. Good. It would make things look more normal to her aunt's eyes.

'Did you young people have a nice walk?' she asked, and then, without waiting for an answer, held up her work. 'It's a shawl,' she announced.

'Good gracious. It's half done already,' said Christie.

'Best to have things ready early. You never know...' muttered the old woman darkly.

'But it's not due until July!' exclaimed Christie.

Sassy sniffed. 'It'll come when it's ready; that's what I always say when people ask. How can these doctors know when a child's ready to be born? They talk rubbish. Anyway, being early runs in the family. Your mother was early. You were too. And then poor little Sarah going into that special-care place. I've seen the poor little mites on television, all wired up in those glass boxes.'

'But Sarah wasn't in an incubator, Aunty——'

'Don't talk about it. It's tempting providence!' insisted her aunt, and turned her attention back to the rapidly expanding shawl.

'But Aunt Sassy... I phoned from the hospital and told you everything.'

Her aunt raised her hand. 'Don't remind me. It was awful. All I could think about was the day your poor father phoned from the hospital when you were born... I couldn't take in a word you were saying. I was frightened to death. So just don't mention it!' she insisted, and that was that.

Lucas put his hand on Christie's shoulder. 'Come on upstairs,' he said evenly. 'Take a warm shower and get into some dry clothes. You'll feel better.'

Lucas stayed in the bedroom while she let the warm water course over her. She felt drained. She wanted to cry, but she couldn't even seem to do that. It was all so awful. Lucas didn't love her. She'd always known that, but her foolish hope had never quite died. When they had got married that hope had been rekindled. And yet the more hopeless it seemed, the more earnestly that silly little flame flickered. After this afternoon it should be extinguished completely. Lucas had admitted that he thought so little of her that he'd believed she wanted to destroy their child. She had seen hatred in his face. But still hope burned on. And now she was stupidly thinking that, if Aunt Sassy really thought all those things about doctors, then perhaps Lucas really *hadn't* known when the baby was due... Except that he'd certainly known that she was early. If it had been James Lakey's baby, then it would have been absurdly, impossibly late...

When she emerged from the bathroom, swathed in towels, Lucas was there waiting for her, with a warm wrap draped over one arm.

'Come on,' he urged. 'Get into this. I don't want you catching a chill.'

'Thank you, Lucas. You're very considerate,' she murmured, letting the towels fall away and hurrying into the dressing-gown. She sat on the edge of the bed. There was a pot of tea waiting for her, and he poured her a cup.

'Get into bed and drink this,' he said.

She turned back the covers and swung in her legs. 'Honestly, Lucas, I'm fine. I shan't come to any harm.'

He sighed. 'For goodness' sake, stop protesting, or I shall get annoyed again. I know you hate me doing anything to help you, but we're married now. You're just going to have to get used to it. I used to think of you going through that first pregnancy alone, with no one to make a fuss of you, and it used to crack me up. I blamed him, of course, at the time. Don't you realise how awful it's been, knowing that he wasn't to blame at all, and that it was me that let you work so hard and struggle on by yourself, all those years?'

She sipped at her tea and closed her eyes. 'I'm sorry, Lucas.'

'Oh, stop saying that,' he jeered unkindly. 'Sorry, sorry, sorry. I told you earlier, I'm not fooled. You hated telling me that Sarah was mine—you did it so grudgingly. And then the next day, when I wanted to pamper you and cherish you, you resisted me and pointedly went off to do your work. Look, I know how hard you've worked to bring up Sarah. You've been absolutely brilliant. She's the finest child a man could ask for, and it's all down to you. But don't you understand how awful it makes me feel? Especially when I think of all those times I nearly got in touch with you, and then held back because, of all people, I'd be the last you wanted to hear from. If you were really sorry you'd let me take care of you properly.'

She opened her eyes and looked at him. He meant every word he said. His face was grave. There was no hint of mischief about his mouth. And suddenly that silly flame shot up like a Bunsen burner and scorched her throat.

'I didn't realise. I thought you thought I was a nuisance and too young to do anything properly, and you just wanted to order me around to make life easier for you.'

He groaned wearily. 'Do you mean that, or are you just saying it for effect?' He shook his head, and his dark eyes met hers. There was a note of keen despair in their mahogany depths. 'You married me for Sarah's sake. I understand that. I shouldn't have made you abandon your career, but I wanted so badly to take care of you both—to see *you*, especially, enjoy the freedom to relax after you'd shouldered the burden so brilliantly for so long. And perhaps I shouldn't have let you get pregnant so quickly.' He paused. 'No, I definitely oughtn't to have done that. It was grossly unfair of me to keep the wedding plans secret so that you wouldn't have an opportunity to make sure we didn't start another baby. I've been used to having things my own way for too long, perhaps... But if you only knew how much I wanted it to happen...'

'You...you planned this baby?'

'Yes. I admit it took a fair bit of conniving to make sure you didn't have a chance to visit a chemist's shop before our wedding night, but——'

'Didn't you imagine I'd already be on the Pill or something?'

'I knew you weren't.'

'How could you have known?'

'All that stuff about boyfriends was lies, Christie. I worked that out a long time ago.'

'Oh...'

'When I asked you to let me know when you were ready to make love with me... Well, I had to admit I thought you were very worldly then. And then I packed your clothes... You know, the day before we got married.' He let out a gentle laugh. 'They weren't exactly the clothes of an alluring young socialite—except for one very special dress. God, Christie, you can't imagine how pleased I was to find that dress—and the shoes, too. I'd ordered this pale grey dress—I've got it somewhere—with a jacket and a hat. You know, sort of bridal but restrained. Then when I saw that black dress I'm afraid I just shoved the new stuff in a cupboard somewhere.'

His eyes seemed to shine with a soft luminescence she had never before seen in them. 'That dress... That was how I remembered you that night. It was how I wanted you to look when we got married. And then I found...' There was a sudden catch in his voice. 'I found a bra. You'd mended it, sewn on a new hook and eye. It...it just seemed kind of poignant—and improbable, too. If you were the sort of girl you wanted me to believe you were... Well, it just set me wondering. No more than that at first. And then we got back to this house and I saw how awkward and embarrassed you were. Good grief—you didn't even know what you liked to drink.

Not to mention those pyjamas! I guessed then that there'd only been...well, perhaps a couple. Me and him, of course... Maybe another one. I get so jealous thinking about it I could choke.'

She closed her eyes again. He didn't know how close to the truth he was getting... Should she tell him now? Have it all out in the open? Or had she been right all along—would the knowledge destroy him? She said nothing.

'That's why I decided to save it for our wedding night. I thought it would make it more special. And anyway, I wanted this next child of ours to be conceived firmly within wedlock. But at least I was the first, even if I did anticipate our wedding night by five years...'

'The first...?' she echoed nervously.

'I could tell. The night of the party. It was very...special. And I felt so privileged...' He sighed heavily. 'Anyway. That's past history.'

'But how could you have known?' She had to bite her lip to stop herself saying any more.

'How could I have known? Well, I'm afraid I wasn't as inexperienced as you. It was very obvious, as it happens... Nice. Wonderful, actually... I hope I didn't hurt you, but I was so eager... I kept trying to stop, but I couldn't help myself...'

'No...' she said weakly. 'You didn't hurt me.'

'I expect you were glad when it was over. I mean, it was a sort of hurdle to get out of the way before you charged back to London to meet up with—er—you know...what's-his-name...'

'Lakey.'

'Yes. Lisa said she'd seen his parents and they said he'd become so touchy lately, and was off out all the time... There was some girl he'd met at school... I'd been his age myself once. I recognised the signs. And then Sassy said you'd rushed straight from your father's place to London, and I was absolutely choked with jealousy.'

Oh, dear. Her hand came up to her mouth. 'You thought that I went to him *after* I'd made love with you...?'

Lucas's eyes were suddenly misted with something akin to hurt. One corner of his mouth puckered slightly. 'Look, you were only eighteen. I didn't blame you. I wouldn't *let* myself blame you. You were so young... God knows I had a hard enough time reminding myself of that. You always seemed so old for your years, even when you were just a kid. Different from every other girl I'd ever known.' He let out a short, bitter laugh. 'I thought it was going to kill me, forcing myself to keep away from you—every damned summer. I used to surround myself with women... and then had to spend half my time fending them off! I used to chant in my head, She's a kid...just a kid...just a kid... Hands off. Don't touch.

'I despised myself for feeling that way about you, when you were little more than a child. I used to get so angry with myself every time you came near. I remembered how I'd been at sixteen and seventeen and eighteen...full of life and raring to go. You needed friends of your own age—I understood that. I used to tell myself...' He stopped himself and looked bleakly into her eyes. 'Oh, what's the use? You don't want to hear any of this. You never have. You wanted that creep. You wanted our baby to be *his* baby. And instead you got me, whom you most decidedly do not want.'

He'd thought she was *old* for her age? He'd wanted her? He thought...? He used to think...? Oh, dear...

Christie sat there in stunned silence, holding her cup. Slowly she raised one hand to her mouth and drew thumb and forefinger unthinkingly from one corner to the other. As if she were unzipping something, or pencilling something in that hadn't been there before.

And then her blue eyes sharpened. Her head tilted slightly to one side. A cynical smile captured her mouth.

'Don't I?' she said, very slowly and very sarcastically.

He looked tired. 'No. And don't start lying to me again. It's too dreary.'

'Are you sure that I don't want you?'

'Yes.'

'How come?'

'You told me Sarah wasn't mine.'

'And if I told you that I said that because I didn't want to trap you, Lucas?'

He shrugged. 'Trap me?' He shook his head.

'Oh, so you know *everything* now, Lucas, do you? Well, you may be able to beat me at chess, but that's only because I haven't had all those innumerable, tedious years that you've had to practise in. It doesn't mean you actually know any more than I do. It just means that you're twelve years older than me, Grandpa!'

He eyed her with a furious frown which dissolved into a look of wary suspicion. 'Christie?'

'For your information, Mr Know-it-all, James Lakey kissed me once. That's all. It was before you ever got round to kissing me, and, quite frankly, it was dreadful. He looks like a chimpanzee, and I'm sorry to say he kisses pretty much like one too. I didn't run off to London to be near him.'

Lucas screwed up his eyes and stared at her in obvious bewilderment. 'Christie?' he asked again. 'I was going to...' He stopped himself, and set his hands on his hips and stared at her.

'You want to watch out, Lucas, or you'll end up like your father. He thinks he knows everything, too.' She folded her arms challengingly across her chest.

'You don't mean that.'

'Don't I?' She arched her brows and looked down her short nose. Then she wagged a finger at him. 'So come on. Give. What was it you were going to say?'

Lucas tilted his chin. His eyes glittered and a look of such mischief captured his features that she thought she might have swallowed an apple.

'I was going to say that I was sorry. That you should be free to do that wretched job of yours so brilliantly, and run your own home, and enjoy the special relationship with your child you've spent so much time developing. I butted into your life and changed everything. I was even going to say that if you wanted to move back to the cottage I wouldn't try to stop you. I was, however, going to say that if ever you thought of inviting Mr Lakey to take tea with *my* children you ought first to warn him that I'd probably break his jaw if he accepted.'

'So what's the problem?'

'I've changed my mind. I'm damned if I'll let you do any of that now. You can keep on doing things my way. On one condition.'

'What's that?'

'You go on talking to me the way you did just then...'

'You mean you enjoy having me pour scorn on your extreme old age?'

'Huh. What would you know about it? You're just a kid...' His eyes were warm, and very, very bright.

'Is that all you've got to say?'

There was a dry pause. 'He kisses like a chimpanzee?'

She shrugged. 'I can't be sure. It may turn out to be one of my little lies after all. I've never been kissed by the genuine article, you see, so I've no way of making comparisons. In fact I've only ever been kissed by one other member of the species *Homo sapiens* in my entire life.'

'One?'

'Yes.'

There was a stunned pause and then Lucas smiled very slowly. 'Good lord, Christie. You developed your expertise in keeping warm in bed remarkably swiftly.'

'I'm a quick learner. Which is beside the point. Look, I can't promise to be rude to you all the time. I'm not sure I've got the stamina. So do you want me to move back to the cottage or what?'

Lucas pulled a face. 'I only wanted you to move back when I thought you were hankering after someone—er—more your own age. However, as luck would have it you have been magically transformed into an old married woman, and old married women should stick by their old married husbands...'

He took her cup out of her hands and set it down on the tray. And then he sat down beside her and slipped one hand inside her wrap so that it cupped the heavy fullness of her breast. 'That's better,' he said. 'Keeping my hands off you has been torment. I don't think I'll bother in future. I'll arrange to keep you beside me day and night...'

His face was closing on hers. She felt his cheek prickle against her own.

'It's all right,' she said wryly. 'You can kiss me if you want to.'

'No chance...' he murmured. 'You can save you mouth for talking. You can tell me for a start what you've done with all that milky rice pudding you've been using for brains lately. I'm fond of this house. If I find you've hidden it under the carpet...' He swung his legs up on the bed so that he was lying beside her.

Christie laughed. 'It vaporised with the scorching heat of my desire. Now kiss me, you old devil.'

His fingers curled tenderly around the soft flesh in his hand. His thumb teased her nipple. 'Nope. Not until you explain all this stuff about my lying to myself. Good lord, Christie. That's a terrible thing to say to a man. It could have had a devastating effect on me... It could have unmanned me!'

She wriggled under the covers, feeling his powerful body stretched out beside her. 'It hasn't, though, has it?' she said happily.

'Luckily for you, no. Even so, you really should explain what made you say such an unlikely thing...'

'Later... Please... I can't concentrate on talking right now...'

His mouth came very close to her ear. He let his tongue trace its shape. 'Nor can I...' he breathed. 'Except... except perhaps to say one last thing...'

'Uh huh?' She snuggled up against him.

'I love you...'

Christie clenched her fists and pummelled at his broad shoulders. 'Stop kissing me...' she mumbled against his mouth.

'Why?'

'I've got something to say...'

But her own declaration was made to wait.

MILLS & BOON

Proudly present...

CHARLOTTE LAMB'S
♥ 100th ♥
ROMANCE

This is a remarkable achievement for a writer who had her first Mills & Boon novel published in 1973. Some six million words later and with sales around the world, her novels continue to be popular with romance fans everywhere.

Her centenary romance '*VAMPIRE LOVER*' is a suspense-filled story of dark desires and tangled emotions—Charlotte Lamb at her very best.

Published: June 1994   Price: £1.90

Available from WH Smith, John Menzies, Volume One, Forbuoys, Martins, Woolworths, Tesco, Asda, Safeway and other paperback stockists. Also available from Mills & Boon Reader Service, FREEPOST, PO Box 236, Croydon, Surrey CR9 9EL (UK Postage & Packing free).

MILLS & BOON

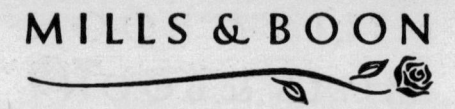

HEARTS OF FIRE by Miranda Lee

Welcome to our compelling family saga set in the glamorous world of opal dealing in Australia. Laden with dark secrets, forbidden desires and scandalous discoveries, **Hearts of Fire** unfolds over a series of 6 books, but each book also features a passionate romance with a happy ending and can be read independently.

Book 1: SEDUCTION & SACRIFICE
Published: April 1994   *FREE* with Book 2

WATCH OUT for special promotions!

Lenore had loved Zachary Marsden secretly for years. Loyal, handsome and protective, Zachary was the perfect husband. Only Zachary would never leave his wife...would he?

Book 2: DESIRE & DECEPTION
Published: April 1994   Price £2.50

Jade had a name for Kyle Armstrong: *Mr Cool*. He was the new marketing manager at Whitmore Opals—the job *she* coveted. However, the more she tried to hate this usurper, the more she found him attractive...

Book 3: PASSION & THE PAST
Published: May 1994   Price £2.50

Melanie was intensely attracted to Royce Grantham—which shocked her! She'd been so sure after the tragic end of her marriage that she would never feel for any man again. How strong was her resolve not to repeat past mistakes?

MILLS & BOON

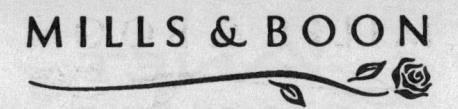

HEARTS OF FIRE by Miranda Lee

Book 4: FANTASIES & THE FUTURE
Published: June 1994   Price £2.50

The man who came to mow the lawns was more stunning than any of Ava's fantasies, though she realised that Vincent Morelli thought she was just another rich, lonely housewife looking for excitement! But, Ava knew that her narrow, boring existence was gone forever...

Book 5: SCANDALS & SECRETS
Published: July 1994   Price £2.50

Celeste Campbell had lived on her hatred of Byron Whitmore for twenty years. Revenge was sweet...until news reached her that Byron was considering remarriage. Suddenly she found she could no longer deny all those long-buried feelings for him...

Book 6: MARRIAGE & MIRACLES
Published: August 1994   Price £2.50

Gemma's relationship with Nathan was in tatters, but her love for him remained intact—she was going to win him back! Gemma knew that Nathan's terrible past had turned his heart to stone, and she was asking for a miracle. But it was possible that one could happen, wasn't it?

Don't miss all six books!

Available from WH Smith, John Menzies, Volume One, Forbuoys, Martins, Woolworths, Tesco, Asda, Safeway and other paperback stockists. Also available from Mills & Boon Reader Service, FREEPOST, PO Box 236, Croydon, Surrey CR9 9EL (UK Postage & Packing free).

JANET DAILEY

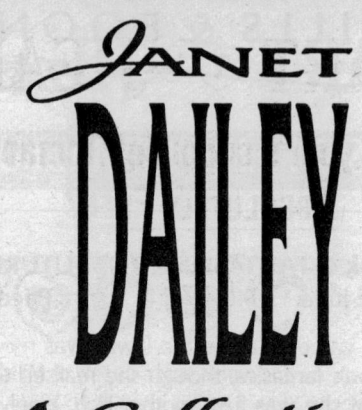

A Collection

Three sensuous love stories from a world-class author, bound together in one beautiful volume— *A Collection* offers a unique chance for new fans to sample some of Janet Dailey's earlier works and for longtime readers to collect an edition to treasure.

Featuring:

**THE IVORY CANE
REILLY'S WOMAN
STRANGE BEDFELLOW**

Available from May   Priced £4.99

WORLDWIDE

Available from WH Smith, John Menzies, Volume One, Forbuoys, Martins, Woolworths, Tesco, Asda, Safeway and other paperback stockists. Also available from Worldwide Reader Service, FREEPOST, PO Box 236, Croydon, Surrey CR9 9EL. (UK Postage & Packing free)

HEART ⓣⓞ HEART

Win a year's supply of Romances
ABSOLUTELY FREE?

Yes, you can win one whole year's supply of Mills & Boon Romances. It's easy! Find a path through the maze, starting at the top left square and finishing at the bottom right.

The symbols must follow the sequence above.
You can move up, down, left, right and diagonally.

START

FINISH

Please turn over for entry details

HEART TO HEART

SEND YOUR ENTRY NOW!

The first five correct entries picked out of the bag after the closing date will each win one year's supply of Mills & Boon Romances (six books every month for twelve months - worth over £85).
What could be easier?

Don't forget to enter your name and address in the space below then put this page in an envelope and post it today (you don't need a stamp).
Competition closes 31st November 1994.

HEART TO HEART Competition
FREEPOST
P.O. Box 236
Croydon
Surrey CR9 9EL

Are you a Reader Service subscriber?   Yes ☐   No ☐

Ms/Mrs/Miss/Mr _____ COMHH

Address _____

_____

_____

_____ Postcode _____

Signature _____

One application per household. Offer valid only in U.K. and Eire. You may be mailed with offers from other reputable companies as a result of this application. Please tick box if you would prefer not to receive such offers. ☐

mps MAILING PREFERENCE SERVICE